FIREFIGHTER DRAGON

FIRE & RESCUE SHIFTERS 1

ZOE CHANT

❀ Created with Vellum

The Fire & Rescue Shifters series

Firefighter Dragon
Firefighter Pegasus
Firefighter Griffin
Firefighter Sea Dragon
The Master Shark's Mate
Firefighter Unicorn
Firefighter Phoenix

All books in the Fire & Rescue Shifters series are standalone romances, each focusing on a new couple, with no cliff-hangers. They can be read in any order. However, characters from previous books reappear in later stories, so reading in series order is recommended for maximum enjoyment.

CHAPTER 1

The first thing Virginia Jones had learned in her very first lecture as a college student was that *real* archaeology was nothing like archaeology in the movies. "We do not," her professor had declared as he swept the rows of eager young faces with a withering stare, "break into foreign locations with crowbars and dodge deadly traps in order to find lost golden treasures."

If he could see me now, Virginia thought with black humor as she levered the crowbar, *the old man would have an aneurysm.*

Admittedly, the foreign location was a construction site in the south of England, and the deadly traps were a couple of CCTV cameras, but Virginia was pretty sure her old professor would still have disapproved. Particularly as she was technically—OK, *very definitely*—breaking the law. Along with the site's side gate. If she could manage to get the stupid thing open.

Next time I have to break and enter in order to protect a site of major historical interest, I'm bringing an angle grinder. Virginia threw her full weight against the crowbar, and was rewarded by the creak of complaining metal as the gate twisted on its hinges. Taking a firm grip on both her nerves and her metal detector, Virginia wriggled through the gap.

In the green static of her rented night vision goggles, the construction site looked like a lunar landscape, with deep ruts and craters where the bulldozers had already scraped back the topsoil. Virginia scowled, anger flooding through her at the sight. Whatever vestigial burial mound might have remained would have been thoroughly destroyed, and precious information along with it. She could only hope that she wasn't already too late to save priceless artifacts from being crushed and desecrated beyond hope of recovery by the uncaring machines.

Checking the compass on her cell phone, Virginia rotated to orient herself. Far below her to the south, she could see the distant lights of Brighton, strung out along the seaside. Up here on the rolling chalk hills of the South Downs, the city looked like a glittering handful of jewels in a cupped palm.

An image of what it would have looked like over a thousand years ago flashed through her head—just a few tiny sparks from the hearths of the Saxon settlers, surrounded by vast, forested darkness. Had one of those settlers looked up at the looming hills where she now stood, and planned how he would be buried there so that he could watch over his descendants as they multiplied in the new home they had named after him...?

"I hope so," Virginia muttered to herself.

Unslinging her metal detector, she set to work. The chalky soil slid under her boots as she methodically quartered the site, swinging the metal detector with a steady rhythm. For the moment, she kept out of view of the CCTV cameras that guarded the scattered bulldozers parked at the center of the site. Her heart leapt at every squeal and click in her headphones, only to plummet again as her searching fingers uncovered nothing more than a stray nail or discarded Coke can.

"Come on, Brithelm," she coaxed under her breath, as though a warrior who'd been dead for over fifteen hundred years could obligingly shift his grave into a more discoverable position. "Don't be shy."

Unfortunately, Brithelm continued to be a coy corpse, as her sweep of the perimeter turned up not even as much as a bent copper coin. Virginia eyed the CCTV cameras, wishing that she'd taken a few electronics or computing courses alongside her archaeology major as an undergrad. As it was, her extensive and detailed knowledge of Anglo-Saxon Migrations (AD 400-900) did not provide her with any particular insights as to how to disable a modern security camera. With a shrug, she started sweeping her way across the monitored area anyway. Having spent the better part of three months single-handedly examining every other square inch of the hills above Brighton, she could hardly turn back now.

"Come *on*, Brithelm," she pleaded, each foot of ground covered eroding her hope.

Four years of research, three preliminary papers, two trips to Europe and one nearly-exhausted grant all led to this tiny bit of churned mud. She'd staked her reputation on this find. If there was nothing here—

The metal detector squealed.

Virginia's heart leaped into her mouth, and she dropped to her knees. Carefully locating the source of the signal, she pulled her trowel from her tool belt and started digging. She methodically passed the metal detector from deepening hole to growing pile of earth and back again, testing each shovelful as she dug. Nothing. Nothing. Nothing.

Signal!

Virginia gently sifted the soil through her shaking hands. Her bare fingers brushed metal, and a peculiar, very unscientific thrill shot through her veins. Even before she rubbed off the dirt, she was strangely certain that this, *this* was what she'd been looking for, and that somehow it had been looking for her too.

Though exactly what it was she had found wasn't immediately apparent. The gently-curving piece of metal was as wide as two of her fingers, and about five inches long. Cradling it in one hand, Virginia fumbled with her night vision goggles with her free hand, pushing them up onto her forehead. She took her penlight from her tool belt, clicking on the narrow beam of light, and directed it onto the piece.

"Oh, you beauty," she breathed, as the light illuminated the unmistakable gleam of pure gold.

She turned the piece over. The concave side was smooth, but the convex side was chased in intricately worked patterns. Even through the concealing grime, Virginia could see that the workmanship was exquisite. An enormous domed gem glinted up at her from the center of the piece, the shifting highlight trapped in its heart making it look like the slitted eye of some fabulous beast.

Like...a dragon? Virginia's heart skipped a beat.

"Brave Brithelm, with the dragon's eye," she said aloud in Old English, quoting one of the few handful of surviving texts from the period that referred to the warrior.

Suddenly what she was looking at clicked into place. "The nose guard of a helmet."

She imagined how it would have looked complete, how the jewels and gold work would have crowned the head of the warrior who wore it in a dazzling display of wealth and power. "A bright helm. *Brithelm.*"

"Ah, the indefatigable Virginia," drawled a familiar, amused male voice from behind her, nearly making Virginia drop the precious artifact. She just managed to shove the nose-guard into her pocket before she was pinned in the beam of a flashlight. "Why am I not surprised?"

"Bertram." Virginia stood and turned, her eyes watering in the sudden glare. Even though her heart was hammering in her mouth, she would rather have died on the spot than given her nemesis the satisfaction of knowing he'd startled her.

"What, slumming it out in the field? I thought you liked to leave that sort of thing to us," she made air quotes with her fingers, "'less intellectual dirt-diggers.'"

"Unintellectual dirt-diggers, my dear," Bertram said, his aristocratic British accent making each syllable ring like cut glass. "Do learn to quote sources accurately. It would improve your papers immensely."

He sauntered forward, delicately picking his way over the churned ground. As ever, he was impeccably dressed in a slim-cut pale grey suit that had probably cost as much as Virginia's entire research grant.

He twitched the flashlight's beam down to the hole at her feet, then back up to her face. "My, haven't you been a busy girl."

I didn't hear a car, Virginia realized uneasily.

Bertram looked as freshly-pressed and crisp as if he'd just dropped out of the sky, but she could only assume that he'd been lurking in the shadows the whole time. Had he seen the nose-guard?

She forced herself to keep her hand away from her coat pocket, and her voice light and even. "Have you been following me, or just hanging round here in the hopes I'd turn up?"

"I had a feeling your little wild goose chase might lead you to do something rash." Bertram inclined his head in the direction of the CCTV camera. "I thought it prudent to keep an eye on my father's investment. After all, I did recommend this site to him as an ideal location for his latest hotel. *Such* charming views, after all."

"You knew," Virginia spat, fury making her fists clench. "You knew all my research pointed to this being Brithelm's grave. You aren't fit to call yourself an archaeologist, you, you *vandal*."

"And yet, somehow, all our peers look up to me, and consider you a laughingstock." Bertram brushed a nonexistent speck of dirt off his sleeve, his heavy gold signet ring flashing as he did so. "If I may offer you a bit of free professional advice? Give up this ridiculous love affair of yours with this entirely mythical warrior. Perhaps you could take up a nice, quiet position in a local history museum? You'd make a simply splendid tour guide for schoolchildren."

"I am so looking forward to seeing your face when I present my findings," Virginia said. "I'll make sure the conference organizers reserve you a front-row seat."

Bertram sighed. "Alas, the academic world is so prejudiced. Criminals are rarely invited to give keynote speeches. Are you aware of the maximum sentence for breaking and entering?"

"Are you aware of the maximum sentence for corruption and bribery?" Virginia shot back. "Because I know you signed off on the paperwork for this site, saying that it was of no historic interest and so suitable for building. And there is no way in *hell* you actually did that survey."

Bertram went suddenly very still. "You found something."

I am alone at midnight in the middle of nowhere with a man who has despised me for nearly a decade, with something in my pocket that is both going to professionally ruin him and incidentally cost his family a very, very large sum of money.

"No," Virginia said, unconvincingly.

"You found something," Bertram repeated. His eyes narrowed. "What? A mere trifle, no doubt. A coin, or an arrowhead. Nothing of significance."

"Hah! You wish." Virginia couldn't help the grin that spread over her face. "Oh, you are so busted, Bertram. This isn't just any old burial mound. This is *Brithelm's* burial mound, and I can prove it."

"You found proof?" Strangely, he sounded exultant. "You must have found...*it*." A hungry expression spread over his face as he took a step closer. "Give it to me. Now."

Virginia backed away, fumbling for her crowbar. "Lay one finger on me and I swear I will brain you."

"Are you threatening me?" Bertram chuckled. "How entertaining. I think that I would very much like to see you try it." He kept coming forward, and Virginia kept retreating. "Come on, my dear delectable Virginia. Don't be ridiculous. You have never been able to win against me, and you certainly won't now. Just give me Brithelm's gem."

Virginia's palm was sweating on the handle of the crowbar. "You'll have to prize it out of my cold, dead fingers, you bastard."

Bertram's eyes glittered oddly in the light. "Excellent."

He lunged, and Virginia hurled the crowbar at him. Without waiting to see if it had connected, she whirled and ran, her boots pounding over the rutted ground. Over her own panicked breathing, she heard Bertram laugh, then a strange noise like an enormous tarpaulin flapping in a storm. Then—nothing.

As she wriggled back through the broken gate, Virginia risked a glance behind her. All was dark. Had Bertram switched off his flashlight, the better to stalk her through the night? She half-slid down the sloping hill to where she'd left her Range Rover parked next to the road, dropping her crowbar in order to fumble frantically for the keys. Expecting at any moment to feel Bertram's hands grabbing at her, she flung herself into the vehicle.

Only when she was finally barreling back down the twisting countryside roads at a thoroughly unsafe forty miles per hour did her galloping heart begin to slow. She drew in a deep, shuddering breath, checking her rear view mirror. No sign of pursuit. Maybe he hadn't had a car. Maybe he'd given up. Maybe he was just—her racing mind scrabbled for ways that rich, evil English aristocrats might deal with people who'd crossed them—on the phone, calmly placing a hit on her.

Okay, now you're just being ridiculous. Giving herself a mental shake, Virginia returned her attention to the road ahead.

There was a dragon in the middle of it.

Virginia had barely even registered the impossible shape when her reflexes took over, stomping hard on the brake and jerking the steering wheel. She had a brief impression of a wall of ice-white scales shooting past the side windows as the Range Rover fishtailed wildly, spinning almost out of control. With all her strength, she clung onto the wheel. In a stench of burning rubber, the car screeched to a halt, facing back the way she'd come. Virginia stared through the steam rising from the hood, her knuckles white on the steering wheel.

There's a dragon in the middle of the road.

There's a dragon.

In the middle of the road.

It's a dragon.

That can't be right.

Shock gave her a strange sense of detachment, as if she was just watching a movie. Everything seemed to go into slow motion, every last detail of the beast searing into her retinas. It was sitting upright like a cat, long white tail wrapped primly around its front—paws? Feet? Huge taloned things? Its horned head was at least twenty feet off the ground. The glowing orange eyes met hers, and the dragon's jaw dropped open slightly, forked tongue lolling out. It looked for all the world as if it was smirking at her.

The dragon unfurled its wings. The lean muscles of its back legs tensed, then it sprang into the air, its wings sweeping downward with a *boom*.

The sound broke her paralysis. She fumbled for the keys in the ignition, her nerveless fingers slipping. Before she could restart the engine, the entire car shook as the dragon thumped into the ground right next to it.

Virginia screamed as the passenger-side window shattered. She hurled herself out of the driver-side door as two sharp ivory talons thrust into the compartment. Then she was sprinting, running faster than she had ever run before in her life, away from the sounds of tortured metal as the dragon tore her vehicle apart behind her.

The loud *boom* rang out again. Virginia whimpered in terror, knowing that the dragon had once more taken to the air. Her night vision goggles chafed her sweating forehead; without breaking stride, she yanked them down over her eyes. Darkness gave way to a flat, monochrome green world. She was in an overgrown field, weeds catching at her jeans as she ran.

A whistle of wind at the back of her neck gave her the barest hint of warning. Virginia flung herself flat as the dragon's talons snapped shut inches above her. Being so large, it couldn't immediately turn back and grab her. It sailed onwards and upwards, the wake of its passing blowing a heavy, animal reek into Virginia's face.

Virginia cast around wildly for any sort of shelter. There was a cluster of barns at the far end of the field—clearly dark and unoccupied, but better than nothing. Virginia ran for them, the downdraft from the dragon's wings cold on her back and neck. She just managed to fling herself into the nearest barn just as the dragon swooped down for another pass. She heard a hiss of frustration as it was forced to veer off again, wings beating hard to avoid crashing into the roof. She slammed the door that she'd come through shut, forcing rusted bolts home.

Got to find somewhere to hide.

To her relief, the barn was an old but sturdy structure, made out of thick wooden beams and metal cladding. She couldn't imagine that even a dragon would be able to easily demolish it. Virginia stumbled between looming, mysterious machinery and piles of boxes, trying to quiet her panicked gasps. A thump reverberated through the ground, as if something very large had just landed outside. Virginia pictured it circling the cluster of buildings, trying to sniff her out.

Trembling, she sank down in the shadows behind a stack of crates. *I've got a moment before it works out where I am. Long enough to call for help.*

She pulled her cell phone out of her pocket, and nearly sobbed in relief when she saw that it had signal. By sheer reflex, she nearly dialed 911 before correcting herself.

"999," said a calm, professional voice in her ear. "What is the nature of your emergency?"

Virginia's mind went completely blank. "Dragon," she blurted out.

There was a momentary pause from the emergency call handler. "Pardon?"

"There's a dragon outside," Virginia whispered. She could hear it pacing outside the barn. It paused, and there was an odd sucking sound, as if it was drawing in its breath. "It's trying to get in."

Another, longer pause. "Do you require fire, ambulance, or police for that, ma'am?"

Outside, the dragon exhaled, and the edges of the barn door lit up with a dazzling orange glow.

"Fire," said Virginia.

CHAPTER 2

*D*ai Drake beat his wings hard, hovering on the night wind for a moment as he scrutinized the South Downs far below. His searching eyes caught on a flickering orange spark near the crest of the tallest hill.

Well, there's definitely a fire, at least, he sent telepathically to Ash. *Can't tell if it's dragonfire unless I get a lot closer.*

Proceed with caution, the Fire Crew Commander sent back. As always, his mental voice was tightly controlled, but from long experience Dai could detect the growing concern under the calm surface of his thoughts. *Dispatch reports we just lost contact.*

Dai hissed under his breath, forked tongue flickering. That meant that the woman who'd made the call, saying she was trapped by a dragon in a burning building, had either hung up or lost consciousness. The rest of his fire crew wasn't far behind, but even with Chase's reckless driving there was no way they could reach the scene as fast as he could.

See you there, Dai sent to Ash, then broke contact. He swept his wings back into a dive, arrowing toward the fire.

Even before he saw the other dragon, Dai knew it was no ordinary blaze. The wooden barn was burning with the white-hot ferocity that could only be sparked by dragonfire. The leaping flames silhouetted a lean, pale form hunched in front of the barn door like a cat in front of a mouse hole.

Anger rose in Dai's chest, and he had to swallow his own dragon-fire. He roared instead, hurling a thought into the stranger's mind like a javelin. *Stop!*

The white dragon leapt, wings twitching open and head snapping round. The stranger's startlement lasted barely an instant, however, before his wings and tail settled into a posture of offended dignity.

How dare you! His mental tone was as rich as gold, and imbued with an absolute sense of his own power and righteousness. His snout turned upwards disdainfully at the sight of Dai's own crimson scales. *Some peasant Welsh red, interfering in my business? Who do you think you are?*

Firefighter Daifydd Drake, of the East Sussex Fire and Rescue Service, Dai shot back as he backwinged in to land. He drew himself up to his full height, glaring down at the white dragon. *Stand aside, now!*

You can't possibly challenge me. The other dragon's head spines bristled in indignation. *Don't you know who I am?*

Yes, Dai replied. The other dragon squawked as Dai lashed out with his muscular tail, knocking the smaller dragon clean off his feet. *You're in my way.*

Before the other dragon could recover, Dai shoved past him. Much as his own inner dragon wanted to formally challenge the arrogant bastard, there was no time for it. He appraised the burning barn with a single practiced glance. There was no way he could enter in dragon form without bringing the whole lot down on the heads of both himself and whoever was in there.

He shifted back into human form. Even as the other dragon struggled back upright, hissing with outrage, Dai ducked through the burning door.

Immediately flames surrounded him, licking at his skin—but the only fire a dragon-shifter needed to fear, even when in human form, was that which came directly from the jaws of a rival. This blaze had been started by dragonfire, but now the flames were just fueled by ordinary wood and air, and so couldn't harm him. Dai still wore the standard protective gear of a firefighter, but it was more for the look of the thing than any real need.

He drew in a breath, the heavy smoke passing easily through his lungs, guiltily savoring the tang of it like an ex-smoker sneaking just one puff from a friend's cigarette. The fire called to his dragon, beguiling in its beauty and power.

Pushing down the instinctive urge to luxuriate in the flames, Dai ducked to peer through the thinner smoke near the floor. "Fire and Rescue," he shouted. "Can anyone hear me?"

That woman is my rightful prey! The other dragon shoved his head through the door, the burning wall disintegrating around him. *She's stolen from my hoard. I demand—*

"Get back before you bring the building down!" Dai yelled back as beams snapped and popped warningly overhead. He couldn't burn or suffocate, but even a dragon could be hurt by a collapsing building. Not to mention the fact that there was a human trapped in here. "Or so help me God, I will find your hoard and personally melt it into slag!"

The other dragon narrowed his orange eyes, but grudgingly retreated. Fresh air sucked in through the hole it had made in the wall, making the flames roar greedily. Dai calculated he had barely a minute before the whole thing came down anyway.

Bits of falling debris clattered off his helmet as he searched through the swirling smoke. According to Griff—the dispatcher who'd taken the call—she'd taken refuge near the back of the building, away from the worst of the flames...

Just as he was giving up hope, he found her. She was unconscious, lying full-length on the floor with her face pressed against a crack in the wall. She must have been desperately trying to suck in fresh air from outside as the smoke overwhelmed the building. She wasn't a small woman, but Dai easily lifted her, cradling her limp form against his chest. He hunched over, trying to shield her from the falling embers as he ran for the door.

He burst out into clean air just as the central support beam in the roof gave way with a cataclysmic groan. There was no time to shift—Dai could only hurl himself to the ground, covering the woman's body completely under his own as burning debris sprayed in all directions. Pain pierced his shoulder as a foot-long splinter of wood hit him with enough force to get through his protective gear. Dai didn't flinch. He kept his body between the woman and the collapsing building until the last strut had crashed to the ground.

A sharp talon prodded him on his wounded shoulder. *As I was saying before I was so rudely interrupted—*

Dai had never been so glad to hear the sing-song wail of the approaching fire engine. "If you have a legitimate grievance, you can either take it to the Parliament of Shifters, or have it out with my commander right now." The post-adrenaline surge crash was starting to catch up with him. His shoulder throbbed, and a dozen lesser pains were clamoring for his attention. "If you're feeling *very* brave. He's not very sympathetic to arsonists."

The dragon hesitated, glancing uncertainly in the direction of the siren. He backed up, opening his white wings. *Just remember, the treasure is mine. And I will be back to claim it.*

"Now there's something to look forward to," Dai muttered as the dragon took to the air.

Dai pushed himself up, wincing as the wooden splinter dug deeper into his muscle. With a bitten-off curse, he reached over his shoulder and yanked it out, tossing the red-stained wood away. He could feel blood trickling down his back, but the wound clearly wasn't life-threatening so he dismissed it from his mind. He was far more worried about the woman he'd rescued from the blaze.

She was still sprawled bonelessly, her eyes closed and her rich brown skin flecked with pale ash. Dai crouched over her, checking to see if her airway was clear. To his relief, she stirred at his touch, coughing.

"It's all right," Dai said, slipping an arm under her shoulders to support her in a more upright position as she fought to clear her lungs. "You're safe. Everything's all right now."

The woman opened her eyes. Dai looked into their warm, dark

amber depths, and suddenly, for the first time in his entire life, everything *was* all right.

"Dragon," the woman whispered.

"Yes," Dai said, voice cracking as delight and awe spread through him. Of course, of course his mate would be able to see straight into his soul, recognizing his hidden nature at a glance. Then her eyes flicked away from his, her gaze skittering over the surroundings as a look of panic spread across her face, and he belatedly realized that she'd meant the *other* dragon. "I mean, no! It's all right, the dragon's gone. You're safe with me now."

She clutched at his hand. "You...saw?" Her voice sounded like she was having to drag words out of her throat on rusty barbed wire.

"Don't try to talk." Dai scooped her up, unable to help noticing her stunning, lush curves as he did so. She fit into his arms so perfectly, he never wanted to put her down again.

Cradling her with infinite care, he carried her further away from the fire, out of range of any further debris. He could feel the way she had to fight for every breath, and his own chest tightened in anxious response.

Where ARE you? he sent to Chase, the driver. *I need the crew here right NOW!*

Astonishment rippled back down the mental link. *You* want *me to go faster?* Chase's gleeful laugh echoed in Dai's head. *Well, if you insist...*

Barely seconds later, the fire engine screeched into the farmyard in a blaze of noise and color. Dai could have sworn that the madman actually managed to get the fifteen-ton vehicle to travel sideways round the corner. He had to duck to protect the woman yet again as the truck screeched to a stop in a spray of sharp gravel and dirt. The driver door flung open, and Chase bounced out, his tousled black hair nearly as wild as his grin.

"And it's a neeeew woooorld record!" Chase announced to the world in general, raising his clasped hands above his head as if posing on a podium.

"Out of the way, featherhead," John rumbled as he squeezed his seven-foot bulk out of the rear seats with some difficulty. He crossed the distance to Dai in two long strides, holding out his enormous hands. "Are you hurt, kin-cousin? Shall I take her?"

"I'm fine," Dai replied, reflexively holding the woman closer as his inner dragon snarled at the thought of someone taking her away from him. "I'll look after her. Where's Hugh?"

"Setting up on the other side," said Fire Commander Ash, jumping lithely down from the fire engine. "He's not geared up, so I want him to stay back."

The Fire Commander's dark, calm eyes swept the scene, taking in every detail at a glance. "Daifydd, get the casualty to Hugh. Chase, stay on the radio, warn us when the police are about to arrive. John, let's take advantage of our lack of mundane onlookers. I'll contain the fire. Can you call the rain?"

The other shifter nodded, the charms woven into his long blue braids clinking. "The clouds are melancholy tonight. I shall sing their tears down."

"Good. Let's get to it, then, gentlemen." Turning to face the burning ruins of the barn, Ash flung his arms wide as if to embrace the fire. It leaped unnaturally in response, stretching out to the Fire Commander as if straining to reach a long-lost lover.

Ash slowly brought his hands together, and the fire grudgingly concentrated itself into a white-hot circle. John tilted his head back, beginning a droning hum in his own language as Ash chivvied stray flames back into the herd.

Dai was happy to leave them to it. His own talents lent themselves more to the "Rescue" side of the work, and it always made him feel inappropriately morose to have to put out a perfectly good fire.

"Hugh!" he called, striding round the truck. "I have a casualty for you!"

"Put her down here." Hugh's distinctive silver hair gleamed in contrast to the red fire engine behind him. He'd already unrolled a blanket and opened up a first aid kit.

Dai carefully lowered her down to the ground and stepped back to give Hugh access to the patient, though his inner dragon growled at having to move even an inch from his mate. He forced down the drag-on's possessive instinct as Hugh crouched next to the woman, his intense blue eyes narrowed in assessment.

"Hello," Hugh said to the woman. "I'm a paramedic. Can I help you?" His clipped, upper-class English accent made it sound like he was merely making polite conversation, but Dai knew he was assessing the woman's ability to respond.

"Throat," rasped the woman. "Hurts."

A tiny crease appeared in Hugh's forehead at her tone, and Dai's heart missed a beat. His dragon rose up, desperate to fight whatever threatened his mate.

She's in good hands, he told his inner dragon as Hugh tugged off one of his disposable plastic gloves with a smooth, practiced motion.

Hugh touched the woman's neck lightly. As his bare skin brushed hers, she winced—and so did Hugh. His mouth twisted in a distinct grimace of pain as he slowly slid his hand down from jaw to collar-bone. After a moment, he drew back his hand, flexing his fingers as if shaking out pins and needles.

"Can you tell me your name?" he asked the woman.

"Virginia." She looked startled at her own voice, which was much clearer than before. She drew in a deep breath. "Virginia Jones. Wow, that feels better." She rubbed her own throat, staring at the paramedic in wonder. "How on earth did you do that?"

"Mild irritation from smoke often clears up quickly," Hugh said, his curt tone dissuading any further inquiry. He snapped his glove back on before taking her pulse, expression back to his customary reserve. "Can you tell me what happened, Virginia?"

"Uh." Virginia's brown eyes went from Hugh to Dai and back again. "It's all a bit...confused."

"He knows about dragons too," Dai said. "He won't think that you're crazy."

Virginia let out a brief bark of half-hysterical laughter. "*I* think I'm crazy." She wrapped her arms around her knees, hugging them to her chest. "That monster...it can't have been real. *Dragons* aren't real!"

"Alas, if only that were true." Hugh murmured as he checked her for any further injuries. Catching Dai's dirty look, he added, "You can't deny we'd all be a lot less busy." He sat back on his heels. "Virginia, you don't have any burns, and you don't have a concussion. However, you've gone through a lot of trauma tonight. For safety, I would like to call an ambulance to take you into hospital for observation and any further treatment."

Virginia's hand suddenly flew to her coat pocket, gripping something through the fabric. "No. I want to go home. I feel fine. Can I just go home?"

Hugh sighed. "One day, one of my patients will actually *want* to go to the marvelous temple of modern medicine. Yes, you can go home, *if*," he raised one long finger forbiddingly, "you can call someone to both take you there and take care of you tonight."

Virginia's face fell. "Oh." She rubbed her forehead. "I'll...think of someone."

Can you give us a minute? Dai sent to Hugh.

The paramedic's pale eyebrows rose, but he got to his feet. "I'll go report to Commander Ash. Let me know when you decide what to do." Flashing Dai a curious glance, he left.

"Please, allow me to watch over you tonight," Dai said to Virginia, as casually as he could with his inner dragon roaring in eagerness. "It's not safe for you to be alone, and not just for medical reasons. The dragon threatened to return."

That bothered him. If she'd never seen a dragon before—and clearly she hadn't—how could she have taken something from one's hoard? Had the other dragon been lying? He pushed the thought away; there were much more important matters to deal with now.

Virginia's eyes widened. "It—what?"

"Shh, shh!" Dai grabbed her shoulders as her breathing started to go shallow and panicky. "It's all right. I'm here to protect you."

"From *dragons*?"

"Yes. It's, ah, sort of my specialty."

She stared at him, apparently taking in his uniform. "But you're a firefighter," she said blankly.

"Yes. But I'm also a dragon..."

18

That monster, she had said.

"...hunter," Dai finished.

It *was* true. Just not...the whole truth.

"A dragon hunter." Virginia made a choked hiccup of strangled laughter. "I managed to call a firefighter who's also a dragon hunter. Boy, is it my lucky day. Apart from the dragon, of course."

"Well, it wasn't exactly luck," Dai said, rubbing his thumbs over her shoulders soothingly. She was still looking rather wild-eyed, but at least no longer on the verge of a panic attack. "Our dispatchers know to send the, ah, unusual calls to our crew. We're used to handling this sort of thing. I really can protect you from the dragon."

Virginia bit her lip. She seemed to waver for a moment, then shook her head. "This is crazy. Everything is crazy. I don't even know your name."

"Dai. Daifydd Drake." Dai exaggerated the soft *th* sound of the *dd*— from her accent, she was American, and they always seemed to have difficulty pronouncing Welsh names.

He stuck out his hand. "East Sussex Fire and Rescue. At your service."

Now, and forever.

CHAPTER 3

his is crazy.

Of course, compared to all the crazy things that had happened this evening—finding Brithelm's burial mound, the confrontation with Bertram, the *motherfucking dragon*—inviting a strange man to stay the night seemed positively sensible. Nonetheless, the taxi ride back to her rented apartment was long enough for some of Virginia's shock to wear off, allowing second thoughts to creep in.

Am I being stupid, trusting a man I've only just met?

Virginia knew that she should have meekly gone to the hospital and let the doctors take care of her. But that would mean delaying investigating her find. Virginia once again touched the thrilling weight of the gold nose-guard safely hidden in her pocket and shook her head. She couldn't afford to wait—and it wasn't just to satisfy her own burning curiosity. She doubted that it was mere coincidence that the dragon had appeared after she'd found the artifact.

Virginia was familiar with many dragon legends from across Europe, and a common factor in them all was the great wyrms' lust for gold. Somehow the beast must have sensed her removing the treasure from its hiding place, and come to retrieve it. But how? Virginia mentally added it to the long list of questions to ask Dai later.

She cast a sideways glance at Dai's profile, half-seen in the dim, strobing glow of the streetlights passing by outside the taxi's window. She hadn't even gotten a good look at his face yet, with all the smoke and confusion at the site of the fire.

I don't know anything about this man. Apart from the fact that he'd pulled her out of a burning building, which anyone would have had to admit was a pretty excellent character recommendation.

However, there was still something about the set of his powerful shoulders that projected an aura of danger. Even his tiniest movements seemed controlled, deliberate, as if he had to keep himself tightly in check at all times. He'd opened the taxi door for her as carefully as if he'd been worried he might absentmindedly tear it off its hinges.

Yet despite all that contained strength, Virginia didn't feel the slightest bit uneasy around him. Sitting next to Dai was like huddling next to a roaring campfire—something fierce and dangerous that nonetheless provided life-giving warmth, and protection against the encircling dark.

Virginia shook her head again, more ruefully. *If the paramedic hadn't given me a clean bill of health, I would suspect that I have a concussion.*

The taxi slowed to a crawl, pulling into a street of close-packed Victorian townhouses, and stopped outside her building. Dai was out of the car and opening her door even before Virginia had managed to get her seat belt unbuckled.

"I'll pay the driver," he said, in that lilting Welsh accent that seemed incongruously gentle coming from such a big man. Virginia could feel the calluses on his long, strong fingers as he offered her a steadying hand out of the car. "Do you need help up the stairs?"

"I'm fine," Virginia said, though in truth she had to haul herself up the few steps to the front door.

Her legs had definitely had enough tonight, and were threatening to mutiny from her body. She surreptitiously leaned on the wrought-iron banister as she fumbled for her keys, grateful that she had the ground-floor apartment.

She let herself into the high-ceilinged lounge, and some of the lingering tightness in her chest eased. Even though it was only a temporary rental rather than a home, it was comforting to be in a space of her own. The research papers scattered over the worn sofa were just as she'd left them this morning, back when the world had been a rational place. It felt like an aeon ago now.

Virginia took the nose-guard out of her pocket, eager to see it in decent light. For the second time that evening, she found herself unable to breathe. It made every piece of Saxon gold work she'd ever seen before—even the famous Sutton Hoo helmet—look like cheap costume jewelry.

Down the length of the nose-guard, the thick gold was chased with exquisitely carved spiraling dragons, writhing round small cabochon rubies. A much larger cabochon ruby took pride of place at the top of the piece, which would have placed it centrally on the forehead of the warrior wearing the helmet. The ruby seemed to glow through the dirt veiling it, a rich blood-red with a dazzling six-pointed star captured within its depths.

Virginia bit her lip, glancing out the bay window. The taxi was just pulling away, which meant that Dai would be entering the apartment at any moment. Where he would find her standing with a king's ransom in the palm of her hand...

And I really don't know anything about this guy.

Even if Dai wasn't the sort to be personally tempted by a hunk of solid gold set with precious gems, there was still the fact that he worked in emergency services, alongside the police. Who would already want to be asking searching questions about how the fire started, and why she'd been up on the Downs in the middle of the night in the first place.

If Dai found out about the artifact, he'd probably feel obliged to inform the police, and then they'd find out that she'd been illegally metal-detecting without the permission of the landowner. In the best case, they'd confiscate the artifact, and she'd lose all chance to work on the find.

In the worst case, it would end up in Bertram's hands.

Best if Dai just doesn't find out about this.

Cradling the treasure, Virginia glanced around. Her tools and specimen boxes were set out on the small dining table, where she'd been working on some coins and minor finds from other sites, but that that didn't feel like a safe enough hiding place.

Hearing boots coming down the hall, she dashed into her bedroom and yanked open the drawer of her bedside cabinet. She tucked the nose-guard carefully out of sight behind a packet of tissues, a tube of hand cream, and a box of aspirin. As an extra deterrent to casual snooping, she made sure her favorite vibrator was right at the front.

There. That ought to do it.

"Virginia?" Dai called from the lounge. Virginia heard him shut the door behind himself. "Are you all right?"

"Be out in a sec!" Virginia called back.

She tiptoed into the en suite bathroom and flushed the toilet, just in case he was wondering at her absence. Catching sight of herself in the mirror, she wrinkled her nose at her charred hair and soot-smeared face. Shower battled sleep on her list of priorities...but neither was as important as finally getting some answers. She pulled off her ruined coat, dropping it in a corner as she left the bedroom.

"Dai," she said as she reentered the lounge. "I want to know—"

The words died in her throat.

Okay. I have not just invited a strange man over to stay the night. I have invited an incredibly attractive *strange man round to stay the night.*

Dai had his helmet under one arm, revealing a strong, square-jawed face that made Virginia's tongue stick to the roof of her mouth. A streak of ash cut across his smooth tanned skin, highlighting the perfect planes of his cheekbones. He absently ran a hand through his short, red-gold hair, tousling the loose curls even further as he looked around.

His bright green eyes seemed to take in every detail at a glance, with the casual but sweeping appraisal of some large predator scanning its surroundings for prey. That assessing gaze snagged on the smoke alarm set into the ceiling. He reached up to it, not even having to stretch onto his toes to push the test button.

"Sorry," Dai said sheepishly, as a loud beeping filled the small room. "Professional habit. You wouldn't believe how many people take the batteries out of these." He jabbed the button again to shut the alarm up. He cocked his head to one side, looking down at her. "What were you saying?"

Virginia belatedly realized that she'd just been staring slack-jawed at him. She struggled to recapture her previous train of thought despite the looming distraction occupying a sizable fraction of her lounge.

"Uh. Dragons. Yes. That was it." She cleared her throat. *Down, girl. So the firefighter is hot like burning. He's here in a professional capacity only. His* other *professional capacity.* "Do dragons come into cities?"

The corner of Dai's mouth twisted wryly. "Yes. But we're safer here than out in the middle of the countryside with no witnesses, at least. We—they normally try to avoid attracting attention."

"I should think it's damn hard for a fifty-foot dragon to avoid attracting attention!"

"You'd be surprised. Many dragons can do a sort of mind trick, which stops people from being able to see them."

"Oh good." Virginia collapsed into the nearest chair. She rubbed the bridge of her nose. "Fifty-foot *invisible* dragons."

"Don't worry, it only works on ordinary people." Dai navigated his way gingerly around the furniture to her side, having some difficulty finding space for his large, heavy boots amidst the scattered books.

He made a short, abortive gesture, as if he'd started to put a reassuring hand on her shoulder but had stopped himself. "I can see them. He can't hide from me."

"But it can make itself invisible to me? Even if I'm standing right in front of it?" Virginia shivered. Despite the warmth of Dai's reassuring presence, the thought of something being able to make her *not notice it* made her blood run cold. "Do you learn to resist dragon mind tricks as part of being a dragon hunter? Can you teach me how to do it too?"

Dai shook his head. "It's something you're born with, I'm afraid." He hesitated, shifting his weight from foot to foot. "You have to be...part-dragon. Descended from them."

"Are you telling me that the fifty-foot invisible dragons can," Virginia groped for a politer word than the first that had sprung to mind, "*interbreed* with people?"

"Ah, yes." Dai avoided her eyes, busying himself unfastening his uniform jacket. "Dragons don't always look like dragons."

With a slight wince, he shrugged off the protective jacket. Underneath he was wearing a simple black T-shirt which strained against his upper arms. Braces ran over his shoulders, holding up his fire-resistant pants and emphasizing the hard lines of his muscled chest. He adjusted one of the straps as he spoke. "Dragons are shifters, you see. Most of the time, they *are* people."

Virginia stared at him, for more than one reason. "Let me get this straight. You're saying that dragons can turn into people."

Dai fidgeted, rubbing at one shoulder. "I'm saying some people can turn into dragons."

Virginia did not feel that this was the time to argue semantics. "Whatever. And they sometimes...*mate* with people."

The tips of Dai's ears were turning red. "Quite often. Ah, that is, I mean, often dragons take *a* mate, not that they often mate with lots of—"

Virginia held up both hands to stop him, shuddering in revulsion. "*Please* do not tell me about the sex lives of dragons. I don't even want to think about it."

Dai's mouth opened, then shut again. He looked desperately uncomfortable. "It's not—"

"Seriously, this is the one area where I really don't need details." Something was nagging at Virginia. She frowned, thinking back over the night. She abruptly sat bolt upright. "Bertram!"

Dai looked taken aback. "Pardon?"

"Bertram. Bertram Russell. He's a...sort of professional rival of mine."

Dai glanced down at the maps and papers scattered around his feet, then at the small brushes and magnifying glasses laid out on the dining table. "You're an archaeologist?"

Virginia liked the rather reverent way he said the word. It made a nice change from the raised eyebrows she usually got when she mentioned her profession. "Yes. I specialize in the early Saxon period, particularly tracking migrations across Europe. Anyway, earlier tonight I ran into Bertram at a building site his family owns, up on the Downs. I ended up running away because I thought he was going to attack me, but when I looked back he'd vanished. And then..."

Her stomach clenched at the memory of bone-white claws stabbing at her, and she had to pause for a moment to regain her composure. "Then the dragon appeared."

Dai's mouth tightened into a grim line. "He's the shifter, then."

He fell silent, studying her. Virginia had the uncomfortable feeling that those clear green eyes could read her like an open book. She was certain that he'd noticed the way she hadn't mentioned just why she'd been up on the Downs in the first place. She was mentally scrabbling for an excuse for her night time hike that *didn't* involve a fortune in gold, when Dai spoke again. "Dragons are incredibly possessive."

It was Virginia's turn to blink at the apparent non sequitur. "What do you mean?"

"A dragon always has a hoard. Gold and jewels are irresistibly attractive, especially anything unique or significant in some way. But taking even the smallest coin from a dragon's hoard is like kidnapping one of their children. He'd stop at nothing to get it back."

"I didn't take anything that belongs to Bertram,' Virginia said firmly.

It was technically true, she told herself. The nose-guard, and anything else that remained in Brithelm's burial mound, was part of Britain's cultural heritage. By law, it belonged to the nation, not to whoever happened to own the land it was found on.

Dai let out his breath, looking relieved. "That's good." Virginia felt a twinge of guilt at the way he just took her words on trust, without asking for any details. "It avoids certain...complications with draconic law."

Implying that if she *had* stolen something, Dai wouldn't have been able to stop the dragon from taking it back. It was a good thing Bertram hadn't managed find the artifact first. Virginia felt physically ill at the thought of the artifacts that must be gathering dust in the dragon's hoard. The nose-guard's true value did not lie in mere gold or jewels, but in the hidden stories it contained, waiting to be unlocked by careful study. The thought of Bertram hoarding it away to privately gloat over was unbearable.

"You know, this does explain a lot about Bertram," she mused aloud. "Now I know why he's such a nasty, controlling, sneering bastard. Suddenly, it makes perfect sense. It's because he's a dragon."

All the relief fled from Dai's face, chased away by dismay. "He *could* just be a bastard."

Is he defending dragons? Virginia was momentarily puzzled, until she remembered something he'd said earlier. "Wait. You're a dragon hunter."

"It's something I do, yes," Dai said, cautiously. "But if you're asking me to kill this Bertram—"

Virginia cut him off with a shake of her head. "Tempting, but not where I was going." Her eyes narrowed as she studied him from head to toe. "You said you had to be part-dragon in order to hunt them, right?"

Every muscle in Dai's shoulders tensed. "Yes."

"So *you've* got dragon blood."

Dai looked like a man staring down a firing squad. "Yes."

"Which you're bleeding all over my carpet."

Dai blinked. "What?"

"You're bleeding, Dai!" Virginia launched herself out of her chair as yet more crimson drops joined the spreading stain on the beige carpet. All other thoughts fled her mind at a sudden urgent, instinctive need to make sure he was all right. "Did you get hurt in the fire?"

"Oh, that. It's just a scratch." Dai rubbed at his shoulder again, then looked at the palm of his hand, which was now covered in blood. "Ah. Hm."

"Let me see," Virginia demanded, pulling at his arm.

Dai was so tall, he had to go down on one knee to let her get a good look at his shoulder. His T-shirt was wet with blood, clinging to the curves of his back like a second skin.

28

Virginia gingerly peeled the shredded fabric away, and sucked in her breath at the sight of the puncture wound in the thick muscle of his left shoulder. "Dai, I think you need to go to the hospital."

Dai rolled his shoulder experimentally. His jaw clenched, but he shook his head. "It's all right. I can still use it."

"Yes, because my only concern about the giant bloody hole in your shoulder was that it might affect your dragon-fighting ability." Virginia cast around for something to staunch the bleeding, but everything she was wearing was covered in dirt and ash. For lack of any better option, she grabbed a cushion and pressed it to the wound. "I left my phone in the bedroom. Hold this in place while I go call an ambulance."

"No!" Dai caught her wrist. Despite the speed and suddenness of the movement, his fingers closed gently, just a feather-light touch on her skin. His green eyes blazed with intensity. "I am not leaving you unprotected."

With him on his knees, their faces were only inches apart. This close, she could see all the shades of color in his irises, from dark emerald to leaf-green, with a thin band of burning gold right around the pupil.

Dragon eyes.

She remembered other eyes—orange instead of green, but with that same hidden fire—and couldn't help flinching.

Dai must have felt her movement, because those brilliant eyes darkened. He looked away abruptly.

"I'll be fine, truly," he said, a rough catch in his voice. "I heal quickly."

"Dragon blood?" Virginia guessed, and sighed at Dai's nod. "Fine, have it your way. But at least let me clean that and put a bandage on it."

She twisted out of his grasp, catching his wrist instead. Feeling rather like a tug boat guiding a battle cruiser, she pulled him to his feet, towing him in the direction of the bathroom. "Before any more dragon blood completely ruins my chance of getting my deposit back on this apartment."

CHAPTER 4

$\mathcal{D}$ai had charged into collapsing apartment blocks to rescue children trapped on the top floor, climbing metal staircases even as the treads melted and twisted under his feet. He'd hauled workers out of a blazing chemical factory, holding his breath for agonizing minutes as he ran through clouds of acidic gases. He'd shielded his crew from dragonfire with his own scaled hide, and had the scars to prove it.

The hardest thing he'd ever done was to sit absolutely motionless under Virginia's gentle touch.

The bathroom was so small, he had to kneel practically between her thighs while she dressed his wound. Every accidental brush of her leg or hip against him burned like dragonfire. His inner dragon writhed in ecstatic agony, demanding that he turn and seize her, to carry her away to his hoard and complete the mating ritual. Dai's fingers dug into his knees as he fought for control. He had long practice at containing the dragon's fiery nature, but all his tricks of focus and distraction were useless in the presence of his mate.

The problem was, he didn't *want* to control the dragon. He too wanted nothing more than to explore Virginia's perfect curves, to taste the softness of her lips. The dragon's desire and his own matched and amplified, until every brush of her fingertips against his back was exquisite torture. Only one thing kept him from turning and claiming his mate.

She hates dragons.

Considering all that she'd been through, it was a perfectly understandable reaction. Dai wouldn't have blamed her for being a sobbing wreck. But Virginia seemed to take all the trauma and convert it into an unbreakable inner strength, like a diamond formed under intense pressure. There had been no fear in her face when she'd spoken of the dragon—just revulsion.

If she knew what I was...

Dai hadn't missed Virginia's tiny flinch when she'd looked into his eyes. Subconsciously, the mate-bond attraction blazing between them had given her a glimpse of his inner dragon. And it had revolted her.

I can't tell her. Not yet. Not until she's had a chance to get to know me, see that I'm not like that other dragon. I have to be patient.

His inner dragon thought that this was a terrible idea. His dragon was much more in favor of sweeping away Virginia's objections to dragons by bringing her to peaks of ecstasy, and provided detailed mental images of exactly how this might be accomplished. Dai breathed slowly, counted wall tiles, and was deeply grateful for the triple-layered material of his fire-resistant trousers.

"Okay, I'm done," Virginia said at last, taping the final corner of bandage into place. She tapped his tense shoulder. "I'm sorry, I could tell that wasn't great for you." She sighed. "It's been too long since I last did remote fieldwork. I'm out of practice with my first aid."

Dai wished he could reassure her that his knotted muscles had nothing to do with pain, and everything to do with her proximity. "It felt good," he forced out through the raw need tightening his throat. "I mean, it feels good. Better. My shoulder. Thank you."

"Anytime." He felt her lean back a little, inspecting her handiwork. She ran her hand over the edges of the dressing, checking it was all secure. "I think this will hold for now. But you should get your doctor friend with the magic hands to look at it later." Her fingers absently continued down the line of his spine. "I like your tats, by the way."

Dai's breath froze in his chest. Even if he'd been able to speak, he could hardly have explained that the scarlet scale patterns that ran down his back were natural, not tattoos. Or that they were so exquisitely sensitive to touch, she might as well have just run her fingers directly over his cock.

He shot to his feet, bashing his head against the light fitting and nearly knocking Virginia from her perch on the edge of the bath.

"Sorry," she said, holding up her hands. Her deep brown skin hid any blush, but Dai could tell she was embarrassed. "That was, um, inappropriate of me."

"No, no," Dai managed to gasp out. He unconvincingly rubbed one leg. "Just, uh, cramp. Anyway. You should get cleaned up yourself." Virginia looked down at her charred clothes, a mortified expression crossing her face, and Dai could have kicked himself. "I mean, it's been a long, tough night. You must want to wash and get some rest."

Virginia smiled wryly. "I could say the same to you." She bit her lip. "Um, not to be inappropriate again, but I don't think you should get that bandage wet. Before I kick you out to get cleaned up myself, did you want some, uh, help in the shower?"

His dragon thought that this was an *excellent* idea.

"No," Dai yelped, hitting his head again on the light fitting in his haste to back out the door. "I'll just go—elsewhere. Now."

He caught a glimpse of amusement battling embarrassment on Virginia's face before the door swung closed between them. A moment later, he heard the shower running. Firmly repressing a mental image of water running over her lush curves, Dai went into the kitchen.

A couple of gallons of icy cold water later, he was at least somewhat cleaner, and in better control of himself. His dragon sulked at the back of his mind, coiled sullenly under iron chains of self-discipline once more. Dai ran his fingers through his wet hair, shaking himself like a dog. Virginia was still showering next door, and he would rather have disemboweled himself than knock on the door to ask for a towel.

What about clothes? his dragon muttered snidely.

Dai looked down at his bare chest and fire-resistant trousers, cursing himself as he belatedly remembered that he was only wearing boxers underneath--he'd been on call tonight rather than at the station, and had been asleep in bed when the alarm had gone out to summon his crew. For a moment, he debated just continuing to wear his turnout gear, but he had the feeling Virginia might not appreciate the aroma of sweat and smoke that permeated the uniform.

I'm never going to hear the end of this, he thought in resignation, as he mentally reached out. *Chase? Are you up?*

As always, came the cheerfully lascivious response. *Where are you, my man? We've all been shitting kittens, waiting to hear from you. Who is this mysterious lady friend you ran off with? Is it true she's taken you home? Have you fu—*

Will you please shut up and listen for once? I need your help.

Did your parents not sit you down for the birds and the bees talk? Chase inquired solicitously. *Don't worry, I'm here to hold your hand all the way through. Metaphorically speaking. Of course, if your lady friend is into that sort of thing, I'd be happy to help out non-metaphorically too—*

CHASE! Dai blasted him with a mental roar, cutting off the torrent. *Seriously. I need some clothes.*

There was a brief mental pause. *Sorry, could you repeat that?*

I need some clothes. I didn't bring anything with me.

So sorry, terrible psychic static tonight. Maybe you're going through a tunnel. One more time?

Dai ground his teeth. *How many times have I rescued you from drunken escapades gone terribly wrong?*

About the same number of times that you've lectured me about my wild ways, Chase responded cheerfully. *Hey, do you think you could call me and repeat this conversation? I want to record it on my phone to savor later. I might make it my ringtone.*

Dai rubbed his forehead, wondering whether to try one of the other members of his crew. Unfortunately, John was probably asleep underwater by now, and just the thought of trying to explain his predicament to Commander Ash made him wince. *Are you going to help me or not?*

Not only am I going to help you, I am going to remind you that I helped you every single day for the next year or so. And I'm already on my way. Dai had an impression of wind whistling past Chase's ears as he stretched into a gallop. *Go outside.*

"Virginia?" Dai called. The sound of running water had stopped, and he could hear her moving around the bedroom. "I'm just going outside. A friend is dropping off some things for me. I'll only be a moment."

Without waiting for a response, he let himself out of the apartment, leaving the door ajar behind him.

Whatever Chase's flaws—and they were many—at least he was fast. Dai barely had to wait five minutes before a duffel bag thudded out of the sky like a meteor, narrowly missing hitting him. He glanced up, catching a brief flicker of Chase's black wings occluding the stars.

Thanks, he sent to the other shifter. *I owe you one. Unfortunately.*

The only response was an amused whinny, drifting down from the sky as Chase shot away again. Dropping the mental connection and picking up the duffel bag, Dai went back inside. Virginia was sitting on a chair in the lounge, wrapped in a fluffy bathrobe, drying her hair with a towel.

"I put a blanket and a pillow on the sofa for you," she said, slightly muffled from the depths of the towel. She flipped it back over her shoulder, scrunching her fingers into her glorious halo of dark hair. "Was that your friend? Didn't he want to come in?"

"Just a flying visit." Dai had to look away from the sight of her flushed, damp skin as his dragon reared up again, fighting his self-control.

He busied himself unzipping the duffel bag, and discovered that Chase had thoughtfully packed him a box of forty-eight condoms, prominently displayed on top of the folded clothes. He thrust them into the depths of the bag. "You should go get some rest."

Virginia yawned, getting to her feet. "No kidding. I feel like I could sleep for a week." Nonetheless, she hesitated at the door to her bedroom. "Are you sure you're going to be all right?"

He caught her gaze with his—and this time, she didn't flinch as she met his eyes. "I've got everything I need," he said. A slow smile spread over his face. "You go sleep. I'll keep guard here."

See? he told his dragon. *Patience. Everything's going to be fine.*

CHAPTER 5

*T*he dragon pinned her down. The bone-white claws dug into her chest, the weight of the beast pressing all the air out of her lungs. She could taste the reek of its breath, a foul mixture of carrion and ash. Its glowing orange eyes were filled with cruel delight at her helpless struggles. The dragon's nostrils dilated as it inhaled; the smirking jaw dropped open. Virginia looked into the gaping maw, and saw the burning flames rushing up the dragon's throat, right into her face—

"Virginia! VIRGINIA!"

Virginia fought like a mad thing against the hot weight pinning her to the bed. She raked her fingernails down—skin? Not scales? She gasped for breath, and tasted clean air rather than smoke.

"It was a dream. Just a dream." Dai's soft Welsh voice in her ear brought her fully out of the nightmare. He was lying across her, on top of the bedclothes. "You're safe. You're safe now."

"The dragon." Virginia swallowed a sob, her breathing still harsh and ragged. Tears streaked her face. "I thought it had me—"

"Shh. I know. Just a dream." He eased his weight off her, releasing her wrists. He pulled her up to a sitting position in the bed, steadying

37

her with an arm around her shoulders. "I'm sorry I scared you. I ran in when you screamed. You were thrashing around so much, I was afraid you would hurt yourself."

Virginia leaned gratefully against his chest. She could hear the deep, reassuring beat of his heart. Her own racing heartbeat started to slow in response.

"I should be apologizing to you." She leaned back a little, tilting her head to look up at Dai. The dim light of early dawn filtering through the blinds was enough to show her the red scratches she'd cut into his cheek and neck. Without thinking, she reached up to trace the marks. "As if you haven't already been injured enough in the course of protecting me."

Dai went perfectly motionless as her fingertips brushed his face. Against her side, Virginia felt the hard muscles of his chest tense, although his grip on her shoulder stayed feather-light. Virginia could hear his strong heartbeat speed up, even as the rest of him went utterly still. Heat radiated from him like a bonfire—but it was a good sort of heat, clean and protective.

That heat kindled an answering fire in Virginia's own body. She'd never had such a strong reaction to a man before. Every fiber of her being yearned for him, like a moth drawn to a flame. She wanted to bury her face in the junction of his neck and shoulder, to drive away the memory of smoke in her lungs with his scent. She craved his skin on hers, his body in hers, burning away her nightmares.

Consumed by that desire, she twisted upright to face Dai, and kissed him.

His lips were motionless under hers for the barest moment. Then he made a low moan, deep in his throat. He flung himself into the kiss like a parched man finally finding water after uncounted days alone in a desert. His strong hands twined in her hair. Virginia ran her own hands down his chest, feeling the hot, solid lines of his muscles through the softness of his T-shirt. She tugged up the hem of the shirt, slipping her hands underneath, glorying in the intoxicating heat of his skin. Her fingers traced the line of his spine, over the tattoos she'd seen earlier.

Dai gasped, jerking his head backwards and breaking the kiss. His eyes were wide and dark, just a thin rim of gold and green showing around the edge of his dilated pupils.

"Virginia," he said hoarsely. "We—first—I should tell you—"

"What?" That brief taste of him had only fanned the flames of her desire. She traced the line of his jaw with her mouth, exploring and nibbling, the slight friction of stubble teasing her lips.

"I—" He shuddered as she bit lightly at his neck. His hands clenched in the thin material of her own nightshirt. "Oh God. Later. Virginia, oh, *Virginia.*"

With a quick jerk, he ripped her shirt from her body—literally, as she heard the fabric tear. She would have laughed in surprised disbelief, except that he'd already dipped his head down to her freed breasts. Virginia arched her back at the unbelievable sensation of Dai's tongue spiraling over her nipples.

His fingers slid under her panties, caressing her slick folds. She pulled at his T-shirt, desperate for more of him. He backed off just long enough for her to pull the shirt over his head, exposing his bronzed chest and hard nipples, then bent back to tease her breasts once more. His tongue left trails of fire over her skin. Virginia ran her palms over the taut curves of his shoulders, savoring both the feel of the solid muscles under her hands and the way Dai's breath hitched at her touch.

His strong fingers circled her clit. Somehow, without any guidance, he seemed to know exactly how to caress her. Virginia's hips jerked as her orgasm built into an unstoppable wave. She clung to him as her climax shook her, biting down on his sweat-slicked shoulder to stifle her cries.

"Please," she gasped as the waves of pleasure subsided. Her pussy ached to be filled. She fumbled with the buttons of his jeans, shoving them down over his hips. "Please, now."

Dai groaned, his mouth open and hot on her breast as her hand closed around his thick, hard shaft. "My Virginia." His voice was a deep growl, shaking with his need and desire. "Mine."

He slid his hands underneath her, cupping her ass. His powerful arms flexed as he lifted her, seemingly without effort, and threw her back onto the bed. He jerked off his jeans and boxers. Virginia had only a brief, glorious glimpse of his full naked body before he was on her, his mouth hungrily finding hers as his cock pressed between her legs. She spread willingly for him, thrusting her hips upward.

The broad head of his cock pushed tantalizingly against her opening—and then stopped. Virginia made a wordless sound of protest, but Dai drew back a little. His chest heaved with barely-restrained need as he raised himself up on his arms above her.

"Condoms," he gasped, glancing toward the door.

She couldn't bear the thought of delaying for even a second. "I've got an IUD." She shifted her hips, rubbing her swollen clit against his thick cock as she spoke. "I'll trust you if you'll trust me."

With a groan, Dai seized her hips, thrusting deep into her. Virginia cried out in ecstasy as his rock-hard cock slid into her slick pussy. She raked her nails down his back, wordlessly urging him to pound her faster, deeper. Dai threw his head back, jaw clenched. She could feel him struggling to contain his own climax as his thick cock caressed her most sensitive inner area over and over, again and again, until she clenched tight around him. Virginia's wordless cry as she came was echoed by Dai's own; his fingers dug into her hips, pulling her hard against his thrusting hips as he finally spent.

They both collapsed back on the bed, still joined. Despite Dai's weight on top of her, Virginia felt as light and weightless as ash on the wind, utterly consumed by pleasure.

After a moment, Dai let out a long sigh. "I never want to move." Nonetheless, he rolled, sliding out of her. He spooned her against his chest, curling around her protectively. "But my shoulder's seizing up. Sorry."

"I'll forgive you," Virginia said, without opening her eyes. "Just this once."

He smelled of clean sweat and wood smoke, the heat of his body against her back as comforting as a log fire in the depths of winter. Something snagged at her slowing mind.

"Hey," she mumbled drowsily. "What was it you wanted to tell me?"

If he answered, Virginia didn't hear. She fell into a deep, contented sleep, and didn't dream of dragons.

CHAPTER 6

When Dai had been a young kid still getting to grips with his dragon, he'd been expressly forbidden to practice fire-breathing. Naturally, this had meant he'd regularly snuck out of the house when his parents were asleep to do so. Whenever his experiments had gone terribly wrong—as they had more often than not—he'd always tried to preemptively put his parents in a good mood by bringing them breakfast in bed the following morning. The bigger the field he'd accidentally torched, the more lavish the breakfast he'd prepare. His mother claimed that to this day, the sight of a plate of bacon and eggs brought her out in a cold sweat of dread.

Dai was currently wishing that Virginia owned a bigger frying pan.

He cursed himself as he flipped the bacon. All his good intentions, all his practiced control—it had all gone up in smoke when she'd touched him.

Yes, his inner dragon agreed happily.

In contrast to Dai's grim mood, his dragon sprawled in luxurious contentment, as smug as a cat in a sunbeam. As far as the dragon was concerned, the only thing that was wrong was that he was out here instead of still in his mate's bed. Even now he could be awakening her with kisses, running his hands over the lush curves of her hips—

Dai shook his head, forcibly thrusting the alluring daydream out of his mind. The dragon was a creature of instinct, unable to think beyond seizing what it wanted, but his human half was not so fortunate. He felt like a little kid again, waking up to the consequences of his nighttime transgressions in the cold, harsh light of day.

I should have stopped. I should have told her what I am. She wouldn't have wanted me if she'd known. I betrayed her trust. I betrayed her.

Dai sighed, steeling himself for what he knew he had to do. *I have to tell her. Straight away, as soon as she wakes up. No matter what the consequences.*

He stared down at the frying pan. *Maybe I should make some pancakes too.*

He could tell the instant Virginia awoke by the way his inner dragon was suddenly on full alert, straining eagerly like a dog on a short leash. He heard the bed creak as she stretched, then the sound of her bare feet on the floorboards. He didn't look round, delaying the inevitable moment by as long as possible.

Virginia's hands slipped around his hips, rucking up his T-shirt. All of his stomach-churning dread melted away at the simple warmth of her skin against his.

"I had this crazy dream that I was rescued from a dragon by a hot firefighter who's amazing in bed." Despite her bold words, her touch was a little hesitant, as if she doubted her welcome. "And now it turns out he can cook, too. I hope I never wake up."

"Good morning," Dai said, turning around in her embrace to catch her in his own arms.

With a tiny sigh of relief, Virginia melted against him. For a moment, all he could think about was how right she felt, how perfectly their bodies fit together.

Then his guilt reared up again. *I'm not worthy to hold her. I shouldn't even touch her.*

Nonetheless, Dai didn't release her. He couldn't bear her to think

44

for even one second that he didn't want her, or that she was just some casual one-night stand to him.

"I hope you're hungry," he said into her ear.

"Ravenous," said Virginia. She leaned round him to peer into the pan. "Okay. Let me clarify that 'ravenous' doesn't mean I can eat six eggs. I hope *you're* hungry."

"Actually, yes," Dai said apologetically, releasing her.

Turning back to his cooking, he slid two eggs onto Virginia's plate, and the rest onto his own. Shifting burned a lot of energy. He added the bacon to the plates, having some difficulty finding space for it next to the eggs, fried bread, sausage, and grilled tomatoes. "It was a busy night."

Virginia raised her eyebrows, a teasing smile tugging at her lips. "Due to the fire or the dragon?"

Dai put a finger under her chip, tilting her face up for a long, deep kiss. "Neither," he breathed.

Releasing her again, he picked up the plates. He tilted his head in the direction of the dining table, which was still piled with papers and archaeology tools. "I didn't want to move anything you were working on, so I didn't set the table. Where do you want to eat?"

"Oh, don't worry, there's nothing important out here." Virginia cleared a space by the simple expedient of sweeping an arm across the table, jumbling papers into haphazard drifts. They sat down, and for a few moments were both fully occupied shoveling food.

"Dai," Virginia said, when they'd both taken some of the edge off their hunger. She kept her eyes on her plate. "I have to tell you something. I haven't been entirely honest with you."

Dai, who'd finally worked up his nerve and opened his mouth to say the exact same thing, found himself totally nonplussed. He blinked at her across the table. "Oh?" he managed to say.

Virginia toyed with her fork. "You know last night, when I told you I hadn't taken anything from Bertram?"

It took Dai a moment to cast his mind back to their earlier conversation, what with the much more significant events that had occurred later. "The dragon? Yes. Though he thinks that you did." Virginia looked at him quizzically, and Dai clarified, "I talked to him last night, at the scene. He was, ah, angry." He reached over the table to put his hand on hers in reassurance. "Don't worry, I'll sort it out with him. I'm sure he'll be back in control of his dragon by now, and able to realize he made a terrible mistake."

Virginia bit her lip. "The problem is, I kind of did take something."

Dai sucked in his breath. "Something valuable?"

She nodded. "Not directly from his hoard, mind. But...I found a valuable historic artifact on land that his family owns. Under British law, they'd be entitled to half the value of the find." She paused, then added, reluctantly, "Actually, in this case, probably the total value. I didn't have their permission to be metal-detecting there. Anyway, I was thinking about what you said, that if I'd taken something it would cause 'complications with draconic law.'" She made air quotes with her fingers. "Is this a complication?"

Dai leaned his chair back on two legs, frowning as he thought. The situation wasn't clear-cut. If Virginia had directly stolen from Bertram's hoard, technically Dai would have had to return the treasure or risk being declared a rogue and hunted down by other dragons.

But since the treasure had just been on Bertram's land...it could be argued that the other dragon hadn't actually claimed the treasure itself, leaving it fair game for anyone else, human or dragon. Of course, it could also be argued that the land included any artifacts hidden within it.

Dai had a nasty feeling he knew which way Bertram would argue.

He sighed. "Unfortunately, yes. Possibly." Catching sight of Virginia's frightened eyes, he thumped the chair back down again, leaning across the table to catch her hand. "*No.* No, it's not a complication, in that I am not going to let any dragon lay so much as a single claw on you. I am going to keep you safe, Virginia. I swear to you, I will keep you safe."

Virginia squeezed his fingers. "I know you want to. But safety isn't everything." Her jaw set in determination, though her eyes still betrayed her apprehension. "I'm not giving Bertram my find, even if it means he's going to come after me. But I don't want to put you in danger too."

"Danger is just a standard day at the office, as far as I'm concerned," Dai said with a wry smile. "Don't worry about me. You take care of your job, and I'll take care of mine." Letting go of her hand, he picked up his fork again. "Which is to protect you from dragons."

Virginia pushed bacon around on her plate, frowning a little in thought. "About that. Is Bertram going to keep trying to steal the artifact back, even after I've handed it in to the proper authorities? A find like this is legally classed as Treasure, so it belongs to the nation. Would he try to break into a museum collection?"

"No, I doubt he'd be that foolish. This Bertram might be willing to risk snatching something from you in a deserted field at midnight, but he'd be in serious trouble if he tried to steal from a museum."

Virginia looked relieved. "You have no idea how glad I am to hear you say that. I was starting to wonder how good the British Museum's anti-dragon defenses are."

"Oh, anything in there belongs to the Queen," Dai said around a mouthful of breakfast. "No one is going to interfere with *her* hoard."

Virginia's fork froze halfway to her mouth. "The Queen is a dragon?"

"Um. Probably best if you forget I said that," Dai said. He waved a hand. "Anyway, the point is, dragons aren't allowed to go around smashing their way into museums—or banks or shops, for that matter. The Parliament of Shifters—a sort of government—comes down very hard on that sort of thing. Dragons are too powerful and dangerous to be allowed to run riot."

"So once I've reported my find and had the site properly declared an area of historic interest, Bertram will have to give up?" Virginia asked.

"Unless he wants to find himself branded a rogue. And trust me, he won't want that. My team would have free license to hunt him down, as would all the other dragon-hunters nationwide. He'd have to flee the British Isles entirely."

Virginia beamed. "Then all I have to do is make a few phone calls, and—oh, damn." Her face fell. "It's Sunday. I won't be able to get hold of anyone until tomorrow morning." For some reason, she cast a worried glance in the direction of the bedroom. "That gives Bertram a whole day."

"Then I won't leave your side for a single moment," Dai said firmly. "If Bertram wants your find, he'll have to get through me."

Abruptly, Dai's dragon reared up in his mind, roaring a challenge. At the same instant, the front door flew back on its hinges with an ear-splitting crash, revealing a tall, slender figure in a pale grey suit.

"That could be arranged," said the other dragon shifter.

CHAPTER 7

"Bertram," Virginia spat. Dai was already on his feet, interposing his body between her and the dragon shifter. "What are you doing here?"

"Mainly, being appalled." Bertram came through the doorway as though forced to step into a swamp, glancing around her small apartment with a look of disdain. His nose wrinkled as his gaze fell on Dai. "Really, Virginia? I had such low expectations of your taste, and yet you still manage to disappoint me."

"You are trespassing," Dai said. His voice had dropped into a deep growl, with a distinct feral edge. He stalked toward Bertram, every muscle in his shoulders and arms tense and ready. "I think you should leave now."

Even though Bertram was at least four inches shorter and a good deal lighter than Dai, he didn't back down. Then again, he could turn into a fifty-foot dragon, after all, so Virginia supposed he had no particular reason to be intimidated by the firefighter's greater size. He met Dai's eyes coolly, lifting his chin a little.

"I possess a flawless four carat princess-cut diamond," Bertram said, his own voice holding a hint of contained snarl.

Virginia blinked, but Dai halted as abruptly as if he'd just run into an invisible wall. His back straightened. "I possess an unworked nugget of Gwynfynydd gold, exceedingly fine."

Bertram's lip curled. "Hah. I possess *four* ingots of pure gold, each one a kilogram in weight."

"What's going on?" Virginia asked, looking back and forth between them.

The two men ignored her. They circled each other like cats preparing to fight, eyes fixed on each other.

"I possess a choker containing a dozen matched rubies of exceptional quality, set in platinum," Bertram declared.

"I possess a flawless five carat cushion-cut emerald, surrounded by twenty diamonds, set in gold," Dai countered.

Okay, Virginia thought in bemusement. *Either firefighters in Britain are paid* much *better than they are back home in the States, or there's a lot Dai hasn't told me yet about his family.*

She didn't dare interrupt again. The mounting menace between the two men was almost visible, like a heat haze in the air between them.

Bertram sniffed. "I possess a flawless *eight* carat emerald, mounted in platinum. Are we going to continue to trade mere baubles, or do you have even a single item of *real* worth?"

Dai set his shoulders like a boxer entering the ring. "I possess a silver chalice, set with cabochon rubies and worked with gold, over six hundred years old."

Bertram waved dismissively. "I possess a complete set of ten nested golden bowls, exquisitely chased, which I took myself from the burial chamber of King Cynewulf of Wessex."

"You do?" Virginia exclaimed.

Dai's jaw tightened. "I possess...the torc of Dafydd ap Llewelyn, first Prince of Wales."

"You *do?*" Virginia said again.

"I see." Bertram's eyes narrowed. "And that is your greatest treasure?" His lean form angled forward, poised for Dai's answer.

Dai's own shoulders relaxed slightly, as though he felt he had the upper hand at last. "It is."

"Oh, well then." All the tension went out of Bertram's body. He threw back his head, letting out a disdainful laugh. "I've barely even got started. I have *nineteen* gold torcs, some worn by kings so old their names are barely remembered. I have so many gold and silver coins from barrows, I can sleep on the pile full-length without even having to curl the tip of my tail. Little red, you could not even begin to *imagine* the scale of my hoard. Do you concede?"

Dai's face was rigid. "I concede."

"What on earth is going on here?" Virginia tugged at Dai's arm. He felt like an iron statue. "Dai?"

Dai breathed out, looking down at her. Though his expression was still tightly controlled, some sixth sense told Virginia that he was mentally cursing himself. "You know the way that a lot of animals don't usually straight-up fight each other, because there's too much risk of getting seriously hurt? Like, say, sheep."

"Sheep," Bertram said. "*Really?*"

"In mating season, rams show off their horns to each other," Dai said to Virginia, ignoring the interruption. "The ram with the biggest, most impressive horns gains dominance over all the others. Rams are big, strong animals who could seriously hurt each other in a real fight. Comparing horns lets them avoid that." He gestured from himself to Bertram. "Dragons do something similar, except instead of comparing horns, they compare hoards."

"Thankfully," Bertram murmured, idly turning a hand so that the light flashed from his heavy gold signet ring.

"So the dragon with the biggest, most valuable hoard is the boss?" Virginia said, looking from Dai's unhappy expression to Bertram's smug one and back again. "But...you just have dragon blood, because of your ancestor. Surely this doesn't apply to you?"

"Oh?" Bertram looked sharply at Dai, who glowered back. Virginia had an odd impression of some unspoken communication flashing between them. Abruptly, Bertram laughed again. "Indeed. Dragon...ancestry." A smile tugged at the corner of his mouth. "My. Well, I suppose that *is* true. And you certainly aren't a *proper* dragon."

"Dragons have *very* strong instincts about dominance and

submission rituals," Dai said tightly. "They have to, otherwise they'd all have killed each other off long ago. I can't help having those instincts too."

Virginia's heart sank. "Which means?"

"Which means that I am dominant over him, and he is thus bound to obey me," Bertram said. His smile widened. "For example, I could order him to leave the city, right now."

"Go ahead and try it," Dai growled. He took a step closer to Virginia. "You'll find that there are some instincts even stronger."

"Mm." Bertram's gaze flicked from Dai to Virginia and back again. His lips pursed as if he'd bitten into a lemon. "How tiresome. But it is an inconvenience rather than an obstruction." He tapped his fore-finger thoughtfully against his chin. "Ah, I have it." He pointed at Dai, his tone turning formal. "Daifydd Drake, by right of dominance I lay this restriction on you—while you are in my territory, you must appear as you do now."

"What? Wearing jeans and a T-shirt?" For a moment, Virginia was perplexed—then she realized that Dai probably didn't usually fight dragons with his bare hands. "Bertram, you can't do that!"

"I can, and indeed, I have." Bertram cocked his head at Dai. "Haven't I?"

Dai's face was expressionless, but his green eyes blazed with fury. "You are dominant over me. Don't think that means I won't punch you in the face."

Bertram raised an eyebrow at him. "A threat, from someone who *isn't* a dragon shifter? I suggest it would be wise to keep silent, little red, and let me talk." He cast a sideways glance at Virginia. "Unless you want me to...talk."

Virginia had the nagging feeling that she was missing about half of the conversation. "What's that supposed to mean?"

Dai folded his arms across his chest, fists clenched as though he was having to physically restrain himself from taking a swing at Bertram. "It means we have to hear him out."

"Good boy. I'm so glad we had this little chat." Bertram dismissed Dai entirely with a flip of his hand, turning instead to Virginia. "It may surprise you to hear that I have come to make you a very gracious and generous offer."

"You can shove it up your English *arse*," Virginia said hotly. "No matter what you've done to Dai, you've lost, Bertram. Soon the whole world will know that I discovered Brithelm's burial mound, and that *you* tried to hide it. Your professional reputation will be ruined."

"That is, of course, assuming that the burial mound is still there," Bertram said.

Virginia sucked in her breath. "You *wouldn't*."

"Oh, believe me, I would." Diamonds glittered as Bertram ostentatiously checked his watch. "It is now...11:23 on Sunday morning, which by my reckoning gives me at least twenty hours before you could possibly hope to report your find to the relevant authorities. Meanwhile, I have an entire construction team who is just *delighted* at the prospect of triple pay for working on a Sunday." He gazed contemplatively at the ceiling. "My. How much concrete could they could lay in twenty hours, I wonder?"

"And if Virginia gives you the artifact she found?" Dai said. "That's what this is about, isn't it?"

"Of course." Bertram smiled condescendingly at Virginia. "I am prepared to be magnanimous. I shall trade you the artifact for the rest of the site."

"What?" Virginia stared at him. "You mean, you'd give me permission to investigate it properly?"

"I would immediately halt construction work, and as the landowner give you full access to the land." Bertram spread his hands. "I'll even help you secure the site. We'd announce the discovery of the site together. My reputation will give you at least some degree of credibility, enough to make sure that you secure funding for a full dig."

"In other words, you want to steal the credit," Virginia said. "And no doubt any other valuable artifacts too. Dai's told me how greedy you dragons are."

"Has he now," said Bertram. "How amusing. No doubt that's true when one only has a pitiful excuse for a hoard." He cast a withering glance at Dai. "I, on the other hand, possess so many treasures already, I would be hard-pressed to even *notice* the addition of one more paltry pile of golden grave goods. I merely have a personal interest in the particular piece you removed. It belonged to an ancestor of mine, and has great sentimental value to my family."

"Sentimental value." Virginia snorted. "Right. Nothing to do with the fact that it's a big chunk of—"

"Ah!" Bertram raised a finger. "If I may offer some advice. It would be wise not to discuss the piece in detail in front of your little...friend here."

"Why are you so sure I haven't already shown it to him?" Virginia asked.

Bertram smiled. "Because he did not list it in his hoard when we dueled. And believe me, if he'd seen the artifact, it would be in his possession right now. He's dragon enough for *that*." He straightened, turning to the door. "You have two hours to accept my offer," he said over his shoulder as he left. "I shall look forward to hearing from you."

Virginia looked at Dai, expecting him to indignantly deny Bertram's parting accusation, but he avoided meeting her eyes. A tiny worm of doubt squirmed in the pit of her stomach. Bertram was a liar and a thief, and she knew she should ignore every word he said...but Dai *did* seem to have a lot of dragon instincts. She was starting to suspect that he was trying to hide the full extent of his dragon heritage from her.

She knew with bone-deep certainty that she could trust him with her life...but could she trust him with her gold?

CHAPTER 8

"*I* don't know, Dai. Maybe I should just accept Bertram's deal," Virginia said. Even though Dai was careful to check his pace to match her shorter stride, she still kept dropping behind, as though having second thoughts about following him at all. "One artifact isn't worth the destruction of an entire site. And it shouldn't matter who gets the credit for the discovery, as long as the site is preserved for study."

Dai wished with all his soul that he could smooth the worry from her beautiful face, but he didn't know how to close the distance that had opened up between them since Bertram's visit. She'd been quiet and reserved since the other dragon shifter had left. The new doubt in her eyes when she looked at him tore his heart in half.

"It does matter," he said firmly. With a light touch on her elbow, he guided her down an alleyway so narrow that the eaves of the houses on each side almost met overhead.

They were in the heart of the Brighton Lanes, a warren of ancient, cobbled back streets. The narrow alleys were packed with an eclectic range of tiny shops catering to a range of specialist interests. Everything from antiquarian maps to fetish wear could be found in the Lanes.

And there were a few very private, very discreet businesses for a *very* select group of customers—shifters.

"It's your discovery," he said to Virginia as he guided her through the maze of streets. It was a route so familiar, he could have found his way in pitch darkness. "I'm not going to let Bertram steal either the artifact or your credit."

Virginia shook her head doubtfully, her face shadowed. "But Bertram's made it clear he's top dog. Top dragon." She blew out her breath. "No offense, but your dragon ancestry seems to be more problematic than helpful at the moment."

"Can't disagree with you there," Dai muttered, making his inner dragon lash an indignant tail.

The beast was as agitated as Virginia was subdued. Bertram's command not to shift weighed on the dragon like iron shackles. It writhed against the restraints, but couldn't overcome its own instinctive respect for a more dominant male. The dragon's helpless rage felt like scales scratching the underside of Dai's skin.

"I know you want to help, and I appreciate everything you've already done," Virginia continued. "But I don't see what you can do now. Bertram's got your hands tied."

"I know," Dai stopped in front of a black, iron-banded door, set uninvitingly in an otherwise blank wall. "Which is why I've brought you here."

Virginia looked up at the grimy sign above the door. It was so thick with dust that the full moon painted on it was only barely visible. "To...a pub?"

"Not just any pub," Dai said. He rapped on the door with his knuckles.

"We're closed!" yelled a woman's voice from inside.

"No you're not," Dai called back. It wasn't much of a password, but it sufficed to keep out random passers-by.

The door opened, revealing the round, smiling face of Rose, the pub owner. "Ah, there you are at last," she said, beckoning them in.

In contrast to the plain, forbidding exterior, the interior of the pub was a snug, comfortable haven of polished wood tables and plush velvet chairs.

"All the other lads beat you here. They're waiting upstairs." Rose's kindly gaze fell on Virginia, who was looking around with a startled expression. "And you must be Virginia."

Although Dai hadn't told her anything more than Virginia's name, there was no hiding anything from Rose. She scrutinized both their faces for a mere second, then clasped her plump hands together. "Oh, Dai, I'm so pleased for you."

"Why?" Virginia asked, a perplexed crease appearing in her forehead.

Dai shot Rose a warning look, but she just laughed. "Because our Dai's never brought a lady friend in with him before," she said to Virginia. "And I can already tell you're not one to put up with any of his nonsense."

It was Dai's turn to frown. "What nonsense?"

"Now that would be telling." Rose winked at Virginia. "Which I shall do later, my dear, when you have time. Our Dai is a lovely lad, but he does tie himself up into knots through overthinking things."

"I do not!" Dai protested.

"Ah, you sweet summer child." Rose patted his arm, then gestured at the back of the pub. "The lads are up in the Fire room, of course. Give me a shout if anyone wants another drink." Rose headed off toward the bar, calling back over her shoulder, "*Except Chase!*"

Virginia flashed Dai a wry grin as she followed him through the bar area and up the staircase toward the private rooms. Dai's heart leapt. It was the first time she'd smiled at him since Bertram's visit.

"I take it this isn't an ordinary pub," she said.

"No," said Dai, smiling back at her. He ducked his head to avoid the heavy oak beams. For a shifter pub, The Full Moon had inconveniently low ceilings. "It's for people like me."

"Dragon hunters?" Virginia asked.

"Amongst other things," Dai said. "Dragons aren't the only type of shifter." He opened the door to the Fire room. "And I want you to meet some of them."

CHAPTER 9

My God, Virginia thought in bemusement. *It's full of muscles.*

The small room was decorated in rich shades of red and gold, creating a warm and snug space that would have been perfect for an intimate private dinner. It was entirely unsuited to the sheer volume of rippling beefcake that currently occupied it. Five men were crammed around a circular table, their broad shoulders hunched over their drinks. The moment Virginia stepped into the room, she was pinned by five sets of interested eyes. She froze under the weight of so much focused attention.

"Dai!" A man with black curly hair sprang from his chair, nearly upsetting his drink into the lap of the blond man sitting next to him. He punched Dai playfully in the shoulder, flashing him the widest grin Virginia had ever seen.

"What took you so long?" the man asked in a strong Irish brogue. His bright, dark glance flitted to Virginia, and his smile widened even further. "Forget it, my question is answered." He made an elaborate bow in her direction. "Lovely lady of mystery, it's a joy to lay eyes on you at last. If you ever need any more midnight supplies, consider me forever at your service. I hope you enjoyed the—"

"*Chase,*" Dai rumbled forbiddingly, and the smaller man shut up, still grinning.

Dai turned to Virginia. "This is my fire crew," he explained. There was something oddly shy in his expression, as if he was introducing her to his family. "My fellow fire fighters. Virginia, this is Chase, our driver. He's the one who brought me the clothes last night."

"In that case, thank you," Virginia said to Chase, shaking his hand. Under any other circumstances, she would have thought him tall and muscular, but standing next to Dai he appeared practically lithe. "And thank you for getting the crew to me so fast last night. Any later and I would have been in big trouble."

Chase's eyes brightened. "My pleasure. Always nice to meet someone who appreciates speed. Tell me, have you ever wanted to take a ride in a fire engine?"

Dai took a firm grip on Chase's arm, dragging him away. "*Do not get into any form of vehicle with him. Ever.*"

"Spoilsport," Chase said, as Dai deposited him firmly back in his chair. He folded his arms in mock-petulance. "It was only *one* little crash."

Dai ignored this, gesturing to another man, who was sitting in a corner of the room a little apart from all the others. "You've already met Hugh, of course."

"How could I forget?" Virginia said, recognizing the silver-haired paramedic.

Now that she could see him properly, rather than in the confusion after the fire, she realized that he couldn't be any older than Dai. His fine, elegant features were young and unlined despite his prematurely white hair.

"I'm glad to have a chance to meet you in better circumstances." Crossing the room, she held out her hand to him. "Thank you for, well, saving my life."

"You are most welcome," Hugh said, leaning back a little. His tone was polite enough, but his upper-class English accent couldn't help reminding Virginia unpleasantly of Bertram. He made no move to take her hand.

Dai gently tapped her wrist. "It's nothing personal. Hugh's not really a hands-on sort of person."

"But I am, so let me make up for my colleague's rudeness," said one of the other men, rising. He was stocky, with a mane of shaggy blond hair framing a square, kind face.

His broad, calloused hand enfolded Virginia's in a warm grip. "Griff MacCormick," he introduced himself. "We *have* already met, in a way, though I'll be astonished if you remember me."

There *was* something familiar about that reassuring voice with its light Scottish burr.

"It was you on the phone!" Virginia exclaimed, realizing. "When I called the fire services!" She squeezed his hand gratefully before she released it. "You talked me through what to do, and kept me calm while I was waiting for rescue."

"Ah, wasn't much work for me, what with a brave lassie like you on the other end of the line." Griff smiled at her, laughter lines crinkling around his golden-brown eyes. "I've never heard anyone describe a dragon so thoroughly."

"I think I was in shock," Virginia admitted.

"And this is John Doe," Dai said, continuing the introductions.

Virginia turned, and took an involuntary step backward as she was confronted by a solid wall of muscle. Dai might have made Chase look slender, but the man who'd just stood up made *Dai* look small.

"John Doe?" she said inanely, the man's sheer size temporarily stunning her brain. "Really?"

"I am told it is traditional use-name amongst your people." The giant's voice was so deep, it practically vibrated Virginia's bones. He had to keep his head bent to even fit in the room. Despite his size, he had a handsome, intelligent face, with deep blue eyes that perfectly matched the shade of his long, braided hair. "I fear you would find my true name unpronounceable."

Virginia couldn't help rising to the bait. "I speak seven languages, four of them extinct. Try me."

"Actually, even John can't pronounce his own name," Dai said. "Not above water, anyway." Before Virginia could ask what he meant by that, Dai gestured at the final man, who had been sitting quietly observing all the other introductions. "And last but no means least, this is Commander Ash."

Now I know what they mean when they talk about people being "old souls."

A shiver ran down Virginia's spine as she met the Commander's calm, assessing gaze. Ash couldn't have been more than ten years older than she was, but she had the sense of something ancient behind those dark eyes. He made her feel oddly small, even more than John had.

"Sir," she said respectfully. She looked around at the five men—all different, yet all powerful in their own way. "So...are you all dragon hunters too?"

All five men stared at her for a moment. Then, in perfect unison, they looked at Dai.

CHAPTER 10

"*D*ragon...hunters?" said John.

Just go with it? Dai sent to them all. Normally he couldn't make five mental connections simultaneously, but panic gave him the strength. *I know it's an oversimplification, but—*

Chase snorted. "Oversimplification is kind of the understatement of the century."

"You mean it's more complicated?" Virginia said, understandably under the impression that he was responding to her. "Do you hunt other shifters as well, then? Dai did mention something about that a moment ago."

Griff was shaking his head. "I don't know what Dai's said, but—"

PLEASE! Dai's psychic shout made the other five men wince. *Don't scare her off. She's my mate!*

There was a momentary pause.

Then Chase let out a whoop. "Uh, sorry," he said, as Virginia stared at him. "I just thought of something funny."

"O...kay," Virginia said, edging away from him a little. She turned back to Griff. "What were you saying?"

"I, uh." Griff flashed Dai a glance that said he had a *lot* of explaining to do later. "I...wouldn't exactly call us hunters." He cleared his throat, recovering some of his usual aplomb. "But we do specialize in handling incidents relating to shifters."

"I am curious," Hugh said to Virginia. His pale blue eyes were narrowed. "What exactly *has* Dai told you about shifters?"

"Not that much," Virginia said. "We've mainly talked about dragons, for obvious reasons. About how they're vicious and greedy, driven by animal instincts."

"Yes," Chase said solemnly, clearly fighting a grin. "Yes, they definitely are. Utter bastards, the lot of them." John made a noise somewhere between a cough and a growl, and Chase quickly added, "Just fire dragons, though, of course. *Sea* dragons are majestic and noble and incidentally would never ever even think about punching someone smaller."

"Um, right." Virginia had clearly given up on making sense of anything Chase said, which Dai felt showed her to be an excellent judge of character. "Unfortunately, my problem is definitely with a fire dragon. The one who started the fire that you rescued me from." Her mouth twisted. "I've come to *really* dislike dragons."

Five fascinated stares fell on Dai again. He fidgeted uncomfortably in his chair.

She doesn't know I'm a shifter, he sent, in a very small mental voice.

"What?!" Griff exclaimed out loud. John said something in his own language which was probably the equivalent.

"As I thought," Hugh murmured into his drink.

My friend, you are totally fucked, Chase sent. *And not in the good way. What were you thinking?*

"Uh," Virginia said, obviously baffled by the way everyone's expressions had just changed. "Did...I say something wrong?"

"No," Commander Ash said. "*You* did not." Dai shrank down, feeling about two inches tall as Ash leaned forward, folding his hands on the table. "But it seems Daifydd has neglected to tell you some important facts. Firstly, that *we* are shifters."

"Real shifters?" Virginia flinched back a little. "Not just descended from them, like Dai?"

*What in the name of sweet green apples did you tell *her?** Chase mentally demanded of Dai. *If I'd known you were lying to get laid, I would not have helped you out.* For once, he actually sounded completely serious.

Kin-cousin, this is both unwise and dishonorable. John's sonorous psychic voice undercut Chase's. His face was set in a mask of disapproval. *I cannot take part in your deception.*

The overlapping telepathic communication made Dai's head hurt. "I *was* going to tell her, when I found the right moment," he said, having trouble keeping all the conversations straight. He gestured at John, hoping to forestall any more awkward questions. "John here is another dragon shifter, but a different type of dragon. He's a sea dragon."

"Oh," said Virginia, her usual boldness subdued. She looked John up and down, or rather up and further up. "Um. Majestic and noble, huh?"

A small smile cracked John's stern face. "We like to think so," he said. He tilted his head, the gold hoops that ran up the edge of his left ear glinting. "Although, from my perspective, I am actually a human shifter. My people live in the depths of the oceans. We are born as dragons, and we die as dragons. Very few of us ever walk the land."

As Dai had hoped, Virginia's curiosity overcame her apprehension. She leaned forward eagerly, her brown eyes alight with professional interest. "You have your own culture? Entirely separate from any human culture? How—"

"I'm sure John would love to tell you all about his people, but it'll have to wait for another time," Dai said. Inwardly, a glimmer of hope grew to a flicker. If she was warming to dragons, maybe she wouldn't hate him when he revealed he was one. "In any case, you see now that dragons aren't all bad? Despite Bertram?"

"Hm." Virginia didn't sound convinced. "Sea dragons, maybe." She looked around the table again. "Somehow I'm guessing that you aren't all sea dragons."

"No," said Griff, smiling. "My mother is an eagle shifter." Virginia opened her mouth, but Griff was already moving smoothly on, leaving no opportunity for questions. "Commander Ash is the phoenix. And Chase is—"

"Ooh, ooh, let me," Chase said, bouncing from his seat. He struck a dramatic pose, as if about to recite a Shakespearean soliloquy. "After all, how can mere words convey my full glory?"

"Not in here, Chase!" Dai yelled...but it was already too late.

The room had been crowded enough before. Adding a stallion did not improve matters.

John grabbed for the table, stopping it from overturning, while Hugh and Griff squashed themselves flat against the wall. Dai encircled Virginia in his arms, trying to keep her away from Chase's hooves.

"My God," Virginia breathed. She reached out to stroke Chase's gleaming blue-black neck. He flirted his head, ears pricked, clearly delighted with himself. "You're a horse."

Chase gave an indignant snort. Virginia's jaw dropped open as he spread his wings.

"Enough!" Dai slapped Chase on the withers. "She gets the point, you're a pretty, pretty pony. Now shift back before you destroy the place."

The air shimmered, and the room abruptly seemed a lot bigger. Chase straightened his suit jacket, an unrepentant grin on his face. He winked at Virginia as he sat down again.

Virginia sank back into her own chair as if her knees had given way. "And...you're a phoenix?" she said to Ash, her voice wavering a bit.

"*The* phoenix," Ash corrected, his tone mild. "Forgive me if I do not demonstrate."

"Uh, right. Of course." Shaking her head as if still in disbelief about what she'd just seen, Virginia turned to Hugh. "And you are...?"

"Private," Hugh said flatly.

Dai cleared his throat, breaking the awkward pause. "Anyway, everyone here has special talents. Between us, I'm certain we can deal with Bertram."

He quickly outlined the events of the last day—well, *most* of the events—to the rest of the crew, filling them in on the details of Bertram's threat. "So you see, the first thing we have to do is protect the site, so that Bertram can't destroy it," he finished. He turned to John. "How are the clouds feeling today?"

"Clouds?" Virginia said.

"I have a kinship with water in all its forms," John said to her. He held out a hand, humming a short phrase under his breath. Virginia gasped, jerking her fingers back as a pint of beer ran up the side of its glass and snaked across the table to curl up like a kitten in the sea dragon's palm.

Griff looked mournfully into his now-empty glass. "I was drinking that."

"My apologies, oath-brother." John flicked his fingers, arcing the liquid sphere neatly back into Griff's glass. He looked back at Dai. "In answer to your question, kin-cousin, when I sing the sky your tale, not a single droplet shall fail to grow fat with rage."

"You can control the *weather*?" Virginia said, sounding awestruck.

"No. I merely talk to it." John shrugged one massive shoulder. "But clouds are just water stricken with wanderlust, and are often pleased to hear a voice from home." His teeth gleamed in a feral grin. "You may expect it to become very, *very* wet indeed."

"Which should stop Bertram's builders, at least for today," Dai said. He looked at Virginia. "You said that you could report the find tomorrow?"

She nodded. "As soon as my colleagues in London are back at work. A find of this magnitude needs to go straight to the top, to the Head of the Portable Antiquities Scheme at the British Museum. I've met him before, so he should take me seriously. He'll have the authority to shut down Bertram's building works."

"Why wait until tomorrow?" Chase asked. "Why not send him a message now?"

"I don't know him *that* well," Virginia said. "It's not like I have his private phone number or anything."

Chase grinned lazily. "I wasn't thinking of a phone call. More like a personal courier." He cocked an eyebrow at Commander Ash. "If you can spare me?"

"You're not on call until Tuesday, anyway," Ash replied. "Can you find him?"

"I can find *anyone*," Chase said, with complete confidence. He inclined his head at Virginia. "If the lovely lady would care to write a note, I will personally put it in the hands of the Chief-Digger-Upper by dinnertime."

A corner of Virginia's mouth curved upward. "Okay, now I know what to put as my title on my next business card. Virginia Jones, Digger-Upper."

She took a notepad and pen out of her jacket pocket and started scribbling away, still looking amused. For once, Dai was grateful for Chase's clowning, if it could put a smile on Virginia's face.

"Griff," he said, turning to the dispatcher. "Can you talk to some of your contacts, see if anyone knows anything useful about the dragon shifter? I'd really like to keep track of where he is and what he's doing."

Griff nodded. "I know some shifters in the police. If I drop a few hints that he was involved in the fire last night, we might even be able to get him brought in. What was the name again?"

"Bertram Russell," Virginia supplied, tearing off her note and handing it to Chase. "But be careful. His family's rich enough to buy him out of trouble, and powerful enough to *cause* trouble. They own Russell Development Group, you see."

Chase whistled. "RDG? That isn't small potatoes. No wonder he trumped your hoard, Dai."

"Thanks for bringing that up," Dai muttered, as his inner dragon snarled at the memory. "But it does bring me to the final part of my plan." He took a deep breath, his dragon's shame at having been forced to submit amplifying his own shame at having to ask for this sort of help.

"Commander," Dai said, not quite able to meet Ash's eyes. "This isn't like our usual rogue dragons, the ones I can freely fight. He challenged me in accordance with dragon custom. And..." His throat clenched on the words, but he forced them out. "He won."

"It wasn't a fair fight," Virginia said, and some small part of Dai's anguish was eased by her defense of him. She folded her arms over her chest, scowling. "His family just bought him a lot of trinkets, and he flat-out stole the rest from archaeological sites. It shouldn't give him any power over you, Dai."

"Unfortunately, by dragon law, it does," Ash said quietly. He considered Dai in silence for a moment, his expression unreadable. "You know that my freedom to intervene is tightly constrained."

"Bertram attacked a mundane and committed arson in the process," Dai said. "Doesn't that put him into your domain?"

Ash steepled his fingers. "In the heat of the moment, yes," he said. Dai couldn't tell whether the pun was deliberate. He'd never quite been able to decide whether or not the Commander had a sense of humor. "But the event has passed, and there does not appear to be immediate threat. I cannot trespass into the jurisdiction of the dragons."

Virginia was looking from Dai to Ash, trying to follow what was going on. "So you can't do anything about Bertram?"

Ash shook his head slowly. "Not while he keeps the peace. If he physically attacks you again, however, it will be a different matter. Let us hope it does not come to that." He looked at Dai. "But it if does, I shall be there."

"We all will," rumbled John, to general murmurs of assent.

"Is there anything in particular you need of me?" Hugh asked Dai.

Dai shook his head. "Not at the moment."

"Wait, yes there is!" Virginia interrupted, sitting up straighter. She poked Dai in the arm, glowering at him. "Or have you forgotten the enormous hole in your shoulder?"

"It's nothing," Dai said hastily, as Commander Ash raised an eyebrow in his direction. "She's exaggerating. I'm fine, honestly."

Hugh sighed. "One day," he said, addressing the ceiling, "one, just *one* of my colleagues might finally grasp the subtle distinction between stoicism and stupidity." He rose gracefully from his chair, taking a sealed packet out of his inside jacket pocket. Ripping it open, he extracted a pair of surgical gloves, pulling them onto his hands. "Let me see it, then."

Dai pulled his T-shirt over his head, and was more than a little pleased by Virginia's soft, involuntary intake of breath. He turned his back on Hugh so that the paramedic could peel back the bandages.

"Mm," Hugh said. Dai winced as the paramedic's gloved fingers lightly probed the wound. "For your future reference, Dai, 'fine' is an appropriate descriptor when one does *not* have a severe puncture in the supraspinatus muscle." There was a rustle as Hugh pulled off one of his gloves. "Now hold still."

Dai felt the paramedic's palm brush his skin—but only for the briefest moment. Hugh snatched his hand back with a bitten-off curse.

"Something wrong?" Dai asked, twisting round in concern. Hugh had shown discomfort when healing him before, but never as vehemently.

"Just caught by surprise," Hugh said through gritted teeth. He was gripping his wrist as if he'd put his hand down on a hot stove. His pained gaze flicked briefly to Virginia. "Though I should have guessed." Clenching his jaw, he placed his palm back over Dai's wound. "Now hold *still.*"

A familiar warmth spread through Dai's muscles as Hugh did...whatever it was he did. Despite their years working together, Dai still had no idea how Hugh's talent worked, or even what type of shifter he was. Still, however mysterious it was, it was certainly effective. In less than a minute, the dull, painful throb of the fresh wound had faded to nothing more than a slight twinge.

"That will have to do," Hugh said, sounding dissatisfied. He stepped back, taking out a small packet of disinfectant wipes and starting to clean his hands. "Please try not to injure yourself more seriously, for my sake."

Virginia touched Dai's shoulder herself, sending a very different sort of warmth spreading through his body. "It's almost completely healed." She turned to Hugh, her eyes wide with wonder. "What *are*—"

"Gentlemen, you have your tasks," Ash interrupted, rising. Chairs scraped as the rest of the team reflexively stood up as well, Dai included. "Let us all be about them." His penetrating eyes rested on Dai for a moment longer than was comfortable. "And Daifydd, see that you do not neglect yours." With a small nod to Virginia, he left.

"What did he mean by that?" Virginia asked Dai, as the others filed out after Ash.

Guilt coiled in Dai's gut. He knew *exactly* what Ash had meant. But Virginia was looking so happy, at last reassured that everything would be well...he couldn't bear to snuff out the light in her face so soon.

"My job is to look after you," he said, hating himself for yet another half-truth. "We still have to get through today. I'm not leaving your side."

"Well." Virginia's gaze dropped to his bare torso, and her soft lips curled in a wicked smile. "I'm sure we'll think of *something* to do."

CHAPTER 11

*W*hen I said we'd have to find something to do, Virginia thought, sea-smoothed pebbles shifting under her feet as she trudged after Dai, *I didn't exactly mean a trip to the seaside.*

At any other time, Virginia would have enjoyed the walk along the promenade. She hadn't spent much time in the city itself over the past few weeks, being far too busy hiking the nearby countryside looking for Brithelm's burial site. The sea front was well worth a visit, with the faded grandeur of the old Victorian buildings making a stately backdrop to the cheerfully kitsch stalls and fairground rides that lined the pebbled beach. And, unfortunately, Dai seemed hell-bent on a long, leisurely stroll.

If someone had told me a few days ago that I was going to be given a personal tour of Brighton's top tourist attractions by an incredibly attractive man, I wouldn't have believed them.

Virginia sighed. She watched the play of muscles in Dai's upper arm as he gestured at the pier, only half-listening to his lecture about its history. The breeze blowing in from the grey-green sea rippled the fabric of his T-shirt, flattening it against the hard planes of his chest.

And if they'd told me that I wouldn't be having a good time, I would have laughed in their face.

The problem was, Dai didn't seem to be enjoying himself either. His stride was just a little too quick, constantly hurrying her along, while his continual monologue never gave her a chance to get a word in edgewise. Virginia had a sinking feeling that Dai was taking her on this walk not because he wanted to share his city with her...but because he didn't want to be alone in private together.

After Dai's fire crew had offered their help in thwarting Bertram, Virginia had felt as if a huge weight had been lifted off her shoulders. She'd even dared to start thinking beyond the next few days. In the cozy pub, with Dai at her side, she'd felt so at home that she'd had a brief, crazy, shining daydream that maybe this could be the start of something more.

If they stopped Bertram from destroying the site and she got funding for a proper dig, she could be based in Brighton for months to come. Years, even, if the site was as significant as she suspected. She and Dai could get to know each other properly. And if she played her cards right, she might be able to use the academic renown from this find to get her dream job at the British Museum. And if she did *that*...maybe she and Dai could have a future together.

Sure, there were a lot of ifs there, but for a moment it had all seemed so possible. And then she'd tried to take Dai's hand, and he'd jumped for the door as fast as if she'd tried to taser him. Since then, Virginia had tried a couple of times to casually touch his arm, but he'd always evaded her, not-quite-casually moving away in order to point out an interesting building, charming view, or (in one case) a passing seagull. For whatever reason, he very definitely wanted to keep his distance.

Virginia forced herself to look away from Dai's strong profile. There was no point tormenting herself with memories of running her hands through that red-gold hair, or the feel of those lips on hers.

Last night didn't necessarily mean anything. We were both high on adrenaline and stress hormones. It was just post-traumatic comfort-sex, that's all.

She stared down at the beach, scuffing the sea-worn pebbles with the toe of her boot.

I bet it happens to him all the time. He must rescue a lot of women, from both fires and dragons. No doubt loads of them get overly attached to him. He's a good guy, he must always try to shake them off without hurting their feelings too much.

Well, she wasn't going to cling to him like some stupid damsel in distress, weeping and begging him to love her. She had her pride. Virginia straightened her back, ruthlessly crushing down her disappointment.

I'm about to announce the biggest find since the Sutton Hoo treasure hoard. I don't have time to moon after some firefighter-slash-dragon-hunter, no matter how hot he is. Or sweet, or brave, or kind, or...

A rumble of thunder broke her rather unhelpful train of thought. The sky was darkening with ominous black clouds, rolling in from the sea so quickly that it looked like a cheap special effect.

"Huh," said Virginia, interrupting Dai's monologue about coastal erosion. She shielded her eyes as the wind picked up. All along the beach, people were hurriedly folding deckchairs and packing up picnics. "That storm sure is coming in fast."

"Ah," said Dai, looking up. "John." He seized her hand, and all of Virginia's determination not to let herself fall for him went up in smoke at the heat of his touch. "Run!"

"Why—" Virginia started—and then the rain came.

It was as if someone had scooped up half the sea in a bucket and tipped it out over the city. The raindrops came down so hard and fast they stung like hail. She staggered under the impact, pebbles shifting and rattling under her feet.

Without even a grunt of effort, Dai scooped her up in his arms, hunching over her in a futile attempt to protect her from the downpour. Virginia clung to his neck as Dai sprinted up the beach toward the promenade. The steps up to the top were thronged with people trying to get off the beach; rather than try to force his way through, Dai found shelter at the base of the wall, under one of the high vaulted brick arches.

"Best to wait for a moment for the rush to die down," he said, his breath warm in Virginia's ear. He lowered her to her feet, though his arms still kept her pressed against him, his broad back sheltering her from the worst of the storm. He let out a short, rueful laugh. "I should have brought an umbrella."

"I'm not sure it would have helped." Virginia laughed too, giddy from their wild dash through the storm. "Bertram's goons certainly won't be able to work through *this*."

She was soaked to the skin. She nestled against Dai's muscular body, his closeness warming her to the core. Despite the heat radiating from him, he trembled a little as he held her, as if he himself felt chilled. His breathing was deep and even, but against her cheek she could feel his heart hammering in his broad chest.

Virginia leaned back a little, tilting her head to meet his eyes, and found them wide and dark, the irises a thin green band around his dilated pupils. Emboldened by the suppressed fire in his gaze, Virginia reached up to brush his wet hair back from his forehead, her fingertips continuing down to trace the line of his cheekbone. His breath hitched. He caught her hand in his, pressing her palm to the side of his face, his eyes closing as if to better concentrate on the feel of her skin on his.

"Virginia," he breathed.

The rain made a silver curtain across the archway, enclosing them in their own private world. She captured his face between her hands, drawing him down for a long, deep kiss. Fire shot through her blood as his arms tightened around her, his tongue exploring her mouth with hungry desire.

Virginia drew back a little, breaking the kiss, though she kept hold of his head. "Why were you pushing me away this afternoon?"

Dai let out his breath in a long sigh. "Because I've been very, very stupid." He leaned his forehead against hers, eyes still closed. "And I'm terrified that you're going to run away when you find that out."

"I'm not going anywhere. Not if you don't want me to." Virginia slipped her hands down, lacing her fingers behind the back of his neck. "So yes, you *have* been stupid."

"No, that's not it." Dai raised his head, opening his eyes at last. His jaw set, as if he was bracing himself to face something. "I mean, I haven't told you something about myself. Something very important."

Virginia raised her eyebrows. "You mean, that you've been deliberately vague about your 'shifter ancestry' because you didn't want me to figure out just how much of a dragon you really are?" She couldn't help laughing at his utterly floored expression. "Dai, I figured *that* out a long time ago."

He gaped at her, his mouth working as if he was having trouble finding words. "When?" he said at last.

"Oh, round about the time Bertram started playing dominance games. The strength of your dragon side became pretty obvious." She tilted her head at him. "Does it come from your mother or your father?"

"Father," Dai said weakly. He stared at her. "It doesn't bother you? Really?"

Virginia shrugged. "Well, it would if you were a dragon like Bertram." She might have wondered if he *was* actually a full dragon, but Bertram's barbed insults about 'not being a proper dragon' had made it very clear that Dai wasn't a shifter. "But you aren't."

"My bloodline isn't even related to his," Dai said, with great finality. "I can promise you, I am *nothing* like Bertram."

"So." Virginia relaxed against him. "This is me, not running away."

She glanced up at him, a little shyly. He was looking at her as if she was some long-lost, priceless artifact that he'd just unexpectedly pulled out of the ground. The heat in his eyes made her stomach flutter. "What happens now?"

Dai stepped back, taking her hand. "Now," he said firmly, "we get extremely wet. There's something at my house I want to show you."

Laughing, Virginia let him pull her out into the rain. The feel of his strong fingers interlaced through hers was enough to warm her whole body. She felt light with relief, as if only Dai's firm grip kept her from floating away into the clouds.

How could he have thought I'd be frightened if I found out he's half-dragon? As he said, he's not like Bertram, after all.

He's not a dragon shifter.

CHAPTER 12

*D*ai felt oddly shy as he led Virginia up the stairs to his bedroom. He rarely had visitors to his house—his dragon's possessive instincts meant he couldn't relax with anyone else in his private space. Now, however, his inner dragon was coiling itself into eager, anxious knots, desperate to see if their territory would please their mate.

"Oh!" Virginia exclaimed in surprise as they entered the bedroom.

Dai's anxiety eased as she looked approvingly around the light, airy room. Dai's house was small, but he'd converted the entire top floor into one big open space, lit by large skylights set above the bed.

"This is nice," Virginia said. To his amusement, she went straight to the floor-to-ceiling bookcases along one wall, being careful not to drip on the leather-bound volumes as she read their spines. "Vintage atlases and travelogues?"

"They're not particularly valuable, but I like them. Most dragons have some sort of personal collection. My father loved science fiction B-movie posters." His mouth quirked in bittersweet nostalgia. "My mother always claimed to hate them, but she still has them all on display."

He took her hand. "But I wanted to show you something else."

Virginia's eyes sparkled as he drew her over to the bed. "I was hoping you—"

Dai put his thumb on the fingerprint sensor hidden in the headboard. With a click and hiss of pneumatics, glass-topped steel drawers slid out from under the bed, display lights switching on.

"...did," Virginia finished weakly. Glittering reflections from the hoard sparkled over her stunned face. "Okay. I have to admit, that wasn't quite what I was expecting."

"Dragons like to sleep on their treasures, so I had the safe built into the bed. It's a bit more comfortable than a literal pile of gold." Dai fidgeted, trying to gauge Virginia's expression as she knelt to inspect his treasures. "Do you like it? I know it's not much, but—"

"Not much?" Virginia cast him a half-amused, half-shocked glance over her shoulder. "If this is what a dragon considers *not much*, I'm terrified to think of what Bertram's hoard must be like."

She laid a careful finger on the bulletproof glass, over the exquisitely-worked gold torc that took pride of place at the heart of his collection. "Is that what I think it is?"

"The torc of Prince Dafydd ap Llewelyn, yes. A distant ancestor." Dai swallowed, his mouth dry. "Would you...wear it?"

"Oh, no, no, I couldn't." Virginia recoiled, looking as guilty as a child caught eying up a forbidden cake. "An artifact like that shouldn't be handled too much. It should be in a museum, not under a bed!"

Dai had been afraid she'd say something like that. "I know. But...I couldn't give up any of the hoard. It's more than just my dragon's possessiveness, though that's a factor of course." He spread his hands. "These are family heirlooms, collected by generations of my ancestors. They're part of my heritage. Part of who I am."

Virginia bit her lip. "Well...it's not like you personally stole artifacts, like Bertram. And you can't help your dragon instincts." A slow smile crept back onto her face as she shot a sideways look at the torc. "Can I really touch it?"

Dai let out his breath in relief. "I want you to touch it. I want you to touch everything." He drew her to her feet, clasping her tight in his arms. "You have no idea how much."

Virginia's hips pressed against his. "Oh, I have *some* idea." She plucked at his soaking t-shirt. "Shall we get out of these wet things?"

Dai put his hands on her shoulders, taking a half-step back even though he could hardly bear to tear himself away from her deliciously soft curves. "Before we do, there's something else I need to tell you about dragons."

"Oh." All flirtation slid from Virginia's expression, replaced by a distinct wariness. "Uh-oh."

"This one's actually a good thing." *I hope you'll think it is, at least.* Dai took a deep breath. "You remember I mentioned that dragons sometimes take a mate?"

From the perplexed crease between Virginia's eyes, she didn't. "A...mate?"

"Yes. All dragons have one true mate, just one person in all the world who's their perfect partner. The mate bond is unmistakable, and unbreakable. Many dragons never even meet their mate, but those who do recognize them immediately."

He gestured at his own heart. "It's...just a bone-deep knowledge, as simple and instinctive as breathing. Just suddenly being totally sure that you've found her. The one."

Virginia had gone very still. Her wide, dark eyes never left his. "You sound like you're speaking from personal experience," she said slowly.

"I am." Dai took both her hands in his own, holding them as carefully as if cradling a bird. "You're my mate, Virginia. There isn't anyone for me but you, and there never will be. I know this must all sound bizarre to you, and I swear it doesn't bind you in any way—"

"Just one question," Virginia interrupted. She looked down at their joined hands. "This mate bond. Does the dragon's mate feel it too?"

"I—" Caught off-guard, Dai hesitated. He couldn't remember his mother ever mentioning how she'd felt when she'd met his father. He sent a mental query to his own inner dragon, but was met with unhelpful silence. "Actually, I don't know."

"Well." Virginia met his eyes. Slowly, the corners of her mouth curled upward. "I do."

Dai's heart missed a beat. *Does she...can she really mean...?*

Virginia laughed ruefully, shaking her head. "It's kind of a relief to know that I'm not going crazy. I never believed in love at first sight before."

"And now?" Dai breathed, drawing her close again.

"Now I believe in dragons. And you." She smiled up at him. "And us."

"If you really mean that, then there's something I'd like to do." He brushed her hair back from her face, still hardly able to believe that this was really happening. His inner dragon radiated smugness, mixed with both anticipation and a touch of exasperation that it had taken him so long to get to this point. "It's a sort of ritual that seals the mate bond."

Virginia's eyes brightened with interest at the word "ritual." "So your father raised you to be familiar with his culture? I'd love to—"

He bent to capture her mouth, cutting her off. He felt Virginia's lips curve under his own, then she kissed him back, abandoning her academic curiosity for now. His hands went to the front of her blouse. His inner dragon wanted to just rip it off, but he made himself take his time, kissing her with luxurious thoroughness as he carefully undid each tiny button. By the time he slid the garment off her lush shoulders, he was shaking with barely-controlled desire. His trembling fingers skimmed Virginia's glorious curves as he unfastened her bra and let it drop to the ground.

Virginia reached for the hem of his t-shirt, but he intercepted her hands. "Please, let me undress you first," he said, his voice so low it was almost a growl. "I want to do this right, and I won't be able to restrain myself long enough if you touch me."

Virginia nodded wordlessly. With the lightest of touches, he guided her down to the edge of the bed. He drew off her shoes and socks, his thumbs caressing the elegant arch of her instep as he did so. There was no graceful way to deal with the soaking wet jeans that clung to the ample curves of her legs; Virginia stifled a giggle, wriggling her hips to help him as he carefully worked the tight material down her thighs and calves. With the same slow deliberation, he slid her panties off as well.

Virginia ran her tongue over her upper lip. Never breaking eye contact, she leaned back on the bed, letting him feast his eyes on every inch of her.

"And now?" she said, her voice husky.

"Now I want to adorn you." Dai opened the cases as he spoke, filling his hands with gold and gems. "I want to adorn you, and adore you."

He straightened, turning back to offer her the very best of his hoard. "Virginia," he said formally. "I show you my hoard, so that you may judge whether I am worthy of you. Do my treasures please you? Will you accept me as your mate?"

She didn't hesitate for even a second. "I will."

Carefully, he fastened the torc around Virginia's neck. The gold gleamed against her dark skin, lovely and precious--but not as precious as her soft sigh of pleasure, or as lovely as the beat of her pulse in the soft hollow of her throat.

"My Virginia," he said hoarsely, crowning her with diamonds and draping her shoulders with pearls. She held perfectly still for him, allowing him to wind emeralds around her wrists and encircle her fingers with rings of gold and platinum. "My mate." He knelt to slip bangles over her feet, until she glittered from head to toe. He sat back on his heels, breathless at the sight of her, adorned like the goddess she was. "My greatest treasure."

He spread her thighs apart, bending his head to worship her with his tongue. She wound her fingers into his hair, wrapping her legs around him. He licked her with slow, circling strokes until her heels pressed deliciously into his back, her thighs clenching as she shuddered with pleasure.

"Dai," Virginia gasped, when she could speak again. "Oh, please." Her fists knotted in his T-shirt, urging him upward. "Please, I need you now."

He didn't need to be invited twice. Virginia lay back, watching him with desire-filled eyes as he stripped his own clothes off. The sight of her spread-eagled, undone with pleasure and gleaming with gold, drove him out of his mind with desire.

Virginia threw back her head, welcoming him with a wordless cry of ecstasy as he sheathed himself in her with one deep thrust. Her fingers raked down the dragon marks on his back, setting his blood aflame. He moved urgently in her, fast and hard, driven by her mounting moans and his own deep need. Her inner walls tightened around him.

"My mate," he gasped as he lost himself utterly. *My mate!*

And at last, she truly was.

"Dai," Virginia said hesitantly some time later, as they lay bonelessly together in the afterglow. "I feel...something strange, in my head."

Hello, he said down the mate-bond, and grinned as she jumped. He propped himself up on his elbows.

"Sorry," he said out loud. "I forgot to warn you."

"I didn't imagine that, then? I heard you in my mind?"

"It's a dragon thing. We can communicate mind-to-mind with other dragons, and some other types of shifters as well." He ran a finger over the torc around her neck. It had warmed to the exact temperature of her skin, as if the gold had become part of her. It was intensely erotic. "Now that you're truly my mate, in a way you're part dragon too. So I can send to you now."

He'd been concerned Virginia might find all this alarming, but her muscles stayed loose and relaxed underneath him. She hesitantly touched his forehead, a look of wonder in her eyes. "I think...I think I can sense how you're feeling."

"Well, I hope you don't need psychic powers for that." He turned his head to kiss the inside of her wrist. "But yes, the mate-bond gives us a sense of each other." The warmth of her mind was stronger than a summer sun. He wanted to lie there and bask in it forever. "You should be able to talk to me when you want, too."

Why don't you try it? Dai sent.

Virginia got a peculiar expression, as if she was attempting complicated mental arithmetic. Dai could feel her fumbling with the mate-bond, sending waves of random, unformed sensations at him. It was rather like being subjected to a kid trying out an unfamiliar musical instrument for the first time.

After a moment she gave up, shaking her head. "That's *very* strange."

"It'll become second nature before too long." Sensing that she was beginning to find him rather heavy, he reluctantly rolled off her, tucking her close against his side. He buried his face in the curve of her neck, breathing in her delicious scent. "My Virginia. My mate."

Virginia giggled, impishly shifting her glorious backside against his stiffening cock. "You've got to be kidding me. Again? Already?"

"I can't help it." He traced the gold and emerald chains looping her arms. "I'm wild for you even when you're fully clothed. You have no idea what seeing you properly adorned does for me."

"Hmm." To his surprise, Virginia wriggled away from him. He would have been dismayed, but the mate-bond reassured him that nothing was wrong—she'd just made up her mind about something. "Wait here a minute?"

Dai crossed his arms behind his head, all the breath sighing out of him at the enticing sway of her breasts as she got up. "Any longer and I'm coming looking for you."

True to her word, she was back in moments, slipping into the room with a shy expression and something concealed in one palm.

"You showed me yours." A mixture of pride tinged with a hint of nervousness radiated down the mate-bond as she held out her hand, opening her fingers. "It seems only fair that I show you mine."

Dai bolted upright. *"Fuck me!"*

Virginia burst out laughing. "That *was* my general intention, yes."

"No—I mean yes, but—" Dai clutched at his own head, nearly deafened by the roars of his inner dragon. The beast was a storm of flame and goldlust, wings beating frantically.

The jewel, the lost jewel, the Dragon's Eye! Jewel of kings!

A torrent of mental images flooded his mind's eye. Warriors in crimson cloaks, dragon-headed ships plunging across a storm-lashed sea, swords and shields and a dragon-eyed man crowned with gold and rubies...

"Dai?" Virginia touched his bare shoulder. "What is it?"

Dai became aware that he'd hunched over as if hurricane winds were howling around his ears. He made himself uncurl, clamping down on his inner dragon's agitation. He stared at the massive star ruby in Virginia's hand in disbelief. "That's the artifact you found? It's called the Dragon's Eye, and it's important. It belonged to...a king?"

Virginia's eyebrows shot up. "I'm pretty certain it's from the helmet of King Brithelm. He was a Saxon warrior who founded the first settlement here, which eventually became Brighton."

"He was also a dragon shifter." Dai rubbed his forehead, trying to sort through the sudden influx of racial memories. "Maybe the first white dragon in the British Isles. Red dragons are native here, but the white dragons came over from Europe along with the Saxon invaders. No wonder Bertram's desperate to get it. Any dragon who claimed that gem would gain incredible dominance."

Virginia's fingers closed reflexively over the artifact. "Dai, if I could give it to you I would, but—"

"No, no." Dai shook his head emphatically. "It's yours. I won't let my dragon try to steal it from you."

His dragon lashed an indignant tail. *Our mate's hoard is a wondrous as she is. We would never seek to diminish it.* It paused for a moment, looking wistfully through his eyes at the ruby. *Unless she wished to trade...?*

Despite his headache, Dai chuckled under his breath. *I don't think so,* he told it. "Actually, my dragon is very impressed with you. That piece is a spectacular hoard all on its own. You'd have a lot of power and status, if you were a shifter."

Virginia sat down cross-legged on the bed opposite him, turning the artifact over in her hands thoughtfully. "You talk like your dragon half is a separate being to yourself."

"Well, it is and it isn't." Dai hesitated. "If you really want to have a serious discussion about the metaphysical nature of shifters right now, do you mind if we put on some clothes?" He gestured sheepishly at his groin. "It's really hard for me to think straight when most of my blood isn't making it as far as my brain."

Virginia's expression clouded with dismay. "I'm sorry, I killed the moment." She held up the Dragon's Eye. "I intended to ask if you'd like it if I adorned *you*."

"Oh," Dai breathed, as his inner dragon surged up. "Oh, yes. I would like that." From Virginia's brief downward glance and sudden smug smile, she could see exactly how *much* he would like it. Nonetheless, he got up. "But later."

"Why later?" Virginia asked, pouting a little.

He kissed her as he started removing his hoard from her gorgeous body, piece by piece. "Because our bond tells me that you're hungry."

"I am?" Virginia's eyebrows drew down, then she let out a surprised laugh. "I am. And so are you."

"So we'll eat, and talk about dragons, and then..." He kissed her again, more lingeringly.

Despite the temptation to decide that neither of them was *that* hungry, they got dressed, though it took rather longer than strictly necessary. Virginia's clothes were still soaking; she rummaged through his wardrobe, finally settling on one of his dress shirts, which drowned her from neck to knees.

"I feel like a reverse Cinderella," she said ruefully, rolling up the sleeves. "From princess to rags."

"You look adorable," Dai told her, holding out his bathrobe for her. She shot him a dry, disbelieving look as she shrugged into it. He spread his hands, smiling. "Just check the mate-bond if you don't bel—"

DANGER!

His inner dragon's shriek came barely in time. Dai flung himself on top of Virginia as the skylight above them blazed with incandescent flame. The glass barely withstood a second before exploding in a hail of shards, but it was enough time for Dai to make the fastest shift of his life, basic self-preservation instinct overriding Bertram's restriction. Dragonfire washed over his back, scorched his armored scales.

The space was much too small for his dragon form. His sides and tail squeezed agonizingly against the walls for a moment before the brickwork crumbled. The floor gave way, unable to support his sudden weight. All Dai could do was curl in a tight ball of wings and scales around Virginia, desperately trying to shield her as they plummeted.

The impact of hitting the ground made him black out for a moment. When he came to, the first thing he was aware of was Virginia writhing in his grip, her hands shoving futilely at his scaled chest. The second was the crushing weight of the collapsed house. With tremendous effort, Dai forced his wings open, bricks and beams sliding off his back.

He twisted his neck, rain running over his spines and into his eyes as he scanned the sky. Since there was no sign of another imminent attack from above, he painfully uncurled, his tail sweeping through burning debris. He managed to roll to one side just far enough to allow Virginia to wriggle free from his grasp.

Heedless of the wreckage all around, Virginia stumbled back, her huge eyes fixed on him. Her terror and panic beat at him down the mate-bond.

"Dai!" she screamed, looking around wildly. "Dai!"

His heart froze in his chest. *Impossible. She knew, she told me she knew!* Yet there was no trace of recognition in Virginia's expression.

I'm here, he sent urgently to her. He tried to get to his own feet, but fallen beams still pinned his hindquarters to the ground. *Virginia, it's me!*

Virginia shook her head in mute denial, still backing away from him—and then Dai saw what was lurking, invisible to non-shifter eyes, right behind her.

VIRGINIA! he roared, both physically and psychically. He made a desperate lunge, but couldn't reach her. *NO!*

Virginia broke and fled—running straight into Bertram's waiting, outstretched claws.

CHAPTER 13

*V*irginia struggled back to consciousness in a cold, muddy field. Her first thought was: *He's a dragon. Dai's a dragon shifter.*

Her second thought was: *I really wish he were here now.*

The white dragon crouched opposite her, legs and wings folded neatly. With an involuntary whimper, Virginia scrabbled away from it, her back hitting a wall before she'd gone more than a foot. The great burning eyes stayed fixed on her with unblinking fascination, like a cat watching a trapped mouse. The tip of the dragon's tail twitched slightly.

Virginia swallowed hard. "I know that's you, Bertram," she said, her voice trembling despite her best efforts. Her legs had turned to rubber. "And you aren't impressing anyone, so you might as well knock it off. I know you aren't actually going to eat me."

The white dragon yawned expansively, giving her a fine view of teeth as long as her forearm. *What makes you so sure?*

Virginia skin crawled at the oily, slick feel of Bertram's voice in her head. She made herself sit up straighter at least, trying to pull together what dignity she could while barefoot and in a bathrobe. "Because you'd be in a hell of a lot of trouble with the other shifters."

The Parliament of Shifters? Bertram's black, forked tongue lolled out in amusement. *My dear delectable Virginia, shifter politicians are much like politicians anywhere—concerned only with keeping their supporters happy. And my family have been* extremely *generous supporters.*

"I didn't mean the shifter government," Virginia said, hoping she sounded a lot more courageous than she actually felt. "If you don't let me go right now, you aren't going to last long enough to face any formal court of justice. Dai will tear you apart."

Bertram rustled one wing in an unconcerned shrug. *The last time I checked, the little red was occupied with more pressing matters. Such as the house on top of him.*

Virginia's blood ran cold as she remembered her last sight of Dai— his sinuous dragon's body pinned under bricks and beams, battered and broken. Even now, he could be bleeding to death, trapped in the rubble...but the mate-bond was a steadfast, warm presence in the center of her chest. Even though she was too far away from Dai to tell what he was thinking or where he was, she knew that he wasn't badly hurt.

Hugh, she thought in relief, remembering the silver-haired healer with the magic hands. *Hugh and the rest of the crew must have helped him.*

"He's fine," she said defiantly. "And I bet he's already on his way here."

What touching faith. You always did have a knack for rejecting the facts. Bertram cocked his head to one side, still looking amused. *How exactly do you think he's going to find you?*

Virginia risked taking her eyes off Bertram long enough to glance around. She'd blacked out during the terrifying flight, so she had no idea where he'd taken her. They seemed to be in a paddock—behind Bertram, she could see a small group of horses huddling at the far end as far away from the dragon as they could get, though curiously they didn't seem totally panic-stricken by his presence. The wall behind her looked like part of some sort of stable building.

Dusk had fallen, but it wasn't yet fully night, so she must have been unconscious for about an hour. It wasn't raining anymore, so either

John had called off the storm or—more likely—Bertram had carried her well away from Brighton.

How is Dai going to find me?

"He'll find me," she said, and was rather surprised to find that she *did* believe that he would, with absolute faith. "He's my mate, and he'll find me."

Bertram flipped his tail dismissively. *Then I'll kill him.* His jaw dropped in an unmistakable feral grin. *I am still dominant over him, thanks to his pathetic hoard. I can stop him from shifting.* His head snaked down so that they were eye to eye, his slitted pupil the size of her entire head. *Tell me, my dear Virginia, how much of a chance do you think a human stands against a dragon?*

Virginia had a horrible certainty that Dai *would* take on a fully-grown dragon with his bare hands, if it was standing between him and her. *The fire crew,* she reminded herself. *They'll help him. He won't be alone.* "I think, if it comes to you or Dai, I'm betting on him."

Bertram's orange eyes narrowed a little. *Give me the artifact,* he demanded abruptly. *Now.*

Virginia's mind raced. She wrapped Dai's robe tighter around herself, mustering as withering a look as she could manage under the circumstances. "Bertram, I'm wearing a *bathrobe.* Do you honestly think I've got a fragile, priceless artifact in my pocket?"

Twin jets of smoke hissed from Bertram's nostrils. *Where is it?*

Virginia took a deep breath, steeling herself. "Dai has it."

Bertram reared back as if she'd slashed him across the snout with a sword. He roared in outrage, the blast of his reptilian breath flattening her against the wall. *WHAT?!*

"I showed it to him, and he recognized what it was. Like you warned me, he wanted it for himself." She folded her arms across her chest, tucking her hands into her armpits so that Bertram couldn't see how they were shaking. "You're too late, Bertram. With the Dragon's Eye, Dai's got a more valuable hoard than you. *You'll* have to submit to *him.* Just give up now, while you still can."

Bertram growled. Without warning, he snatched her up in one of his front feet, the white claws closing around her so tightly Virginia couldn't even draw breath to scream.

Hobbling awkwardly on three legs, Bertram carried her out of the paddock and into a courtyard surrounded by stable buildings. The complex was dominated by a huge structure, big enough for even a dragon to enter, which Virginia assumed had to be a covered riding arena—until Bertram nosed open the door, and her eyes were blinded by dazzling gold.

My God. And I thought Dai's *bed was over the top.*

Bertram hadn't been kidding about being able to sleep full-length on top of his hoard. The plain exterior of the barn concealed an enormous mound of jumbled gold, silver and gems. An almost physical pain shot through Virginia's chest at the sight of so many artifacts so casually tumbled together. It was a far cry from Dai's meticulously stored and treasured collection.

Bertram's claws raked carelessly through the pile as he clambered over coins and cups to the center of the room. Stretching on his back legs, he dropped Virginia onto one of the steel girders supporting the high A-frame roof. Heart hammering, Virginia clutched at the dusty metal, fighting vertigo at the sight of the floor so far below. There was no question of jumping down, and nowhere to go. She was trapped.

Virginia forced her breathing to slow. Carefully, she straddled the beam, trying not to look down. She concentrated instead on the steady beacon of the mate-bond in her mind.

"Dai *is* coming for me," she said out loud.

The white dragon shimmered, shrinking into human shape. "Indeed." Bertram smirked up at her as he took his cell phone out of his pocket. "In fact, I'm counting on it."

CHAPTER 14

"*I* don't have time for this," Dai snarled at Ash. "I have to find Virginia!"

"If you move again, I will personally break your other bloody leg," Hugh snapped. His bare fingers dug into Dai's calf as his healing talent knit bone and muscle back together. "Do you want to have to crawl to your mate's rescue?"

"If I have to, yes!"

"You don't know where he took her," Ash said. Dai could have throttled the Commander for his level voice and calm expression.

Behind the Commander, another fire crew worked to put out the smoldering remains of Dai's house. Thanks to John's rain and Ash's prompt arrival, the blaze hadn't had the chance to spread to neighboring properties. The police were cordoning off the street, keeping curious onlookers well back.

"Chase is on his way back from London as fast as he can fly," Ash said. "As soon as he's here, he'll be able to lead us to her."

"I can't wait that long!" Dai tried to push himself up, but John's enormous hands on his shoulders kept him firmly seated on the ground. "I can't sit here doing nothing. Virginia needs me *now*." Her fear sawed at his soul through the mate-bond. "If you'd ever met *your* mate, you'd understand!"

Ash looked at him. Though his expression never changed, even Dai's inner dragon recoiled from the brief glimpse of the inferno concealed behind those black eyes.

"I understand very well," the Commander said quietly. "But it does not change the fact that you can do nothing to help her right now."

Dai was saved from saying something potentially career-limiting to his commander by Ash's phone beeping. Ash touched his hand to his earpiece, listening. His eyebrows rose fractionally.

"I see," Ash said. Unclipping the phone, he passed it to Dai. "It's Griff."

"Dai?" Griff's Scottish burr was more pronounced than usual, a sure sign of agitation. "We just got the oddest emergency call here. He called 999 and then asked for you personally. He won't give his own name or location, but I'm certain it's your dragon shifter."

Adrenaline surged through Dai's blood. "Can you trace the call?"

"I'm working on it, but he's on a mobile phone so it's not easy." Dai could hear the rapid rattle of computer keys in the background. "Do you want me to keep stalling him, or put him through to you?"

"Put him through," Dai growled. There was a click as Griff did so. "Bertram?"

"I will offer you this trade once, and once only." Bertram's icy tones struck Dai like a blow. He could practically taste dragonfire rising in his throat in response. "Your mate for the Dragon's Eye."

"I don't have it." Dai glanced over his shoulder at the pile of wreckage that had been his house. "Even if it's still intact, it's buried under a ton of bricks."

Bertram's scornful laugh rang in his ear. "Do you think me a fool? I know she gave it to you, so it must be on your person right this moment. No dragon would have put down such a treasure for even a second. You have thirty minutes to bring it to the site of Brithelm's burial mound. Come alone. If you try to trick me, your mate will burn."

"Wait—!" Dai found himself talking to a dead line. He lowered the phone, his forehead furrowing. He looked up to find the rest of the crew watching him in concern. "Did you all catch that?"

John nodded. "Do you actually have this treasure the crawling worm seeks, kin-cousin?"

"No," Dai said slowly. "And now I'm trying to remember if *Virginia* ever put it down."

CHAPTER 15

*O*virginia's feet were freezing, and she had a cramp in one hand from clinging to the cold metal beam. Bertram seemed to have been gone for hours. With childish malice, he'd flicked the lights off when he'd left, leaving her stranded in pitch darkness.

Virginia buried her face in the soft, worn material of Dai's robe, breathing in the faint trace of his wood-smoke scent to keep herself calm. She knew that he was getting closer. The mate-bond was growing steadily brighter, flaring from a mere ember to a roaring bonfire in her soul. Through it, she could sense Dai's fierce rage and his determination—and also how terribly afraid he was for her.

Just come to me, she tried to send down the mate-bond, over and over. She didn't know whether her words were reaching him. All she could do was concentrate on radiating encouragement and reassurance down their mental link. **Trust me. Come.**

The huge door rattled open again. Virginia squinted as the lights came on again, blinding after the total darkness.

Her heart leapt at the sight of Dai's tall form in the doorway—but Bertram, back in dragon form, was right behind him, prodding him along with vicious jabs of his ivory talons. From Dai's windswept hair and ripped shirt, Bertram must have carried him through the air rather than allowing him to shift and fly himself.

"Dai!" Virginia called out to him. "Up here!"

"Virginia!" Dai rushed forward, but had to halt as Bertram whipped his tail forward to bar his way. Dai struck his fist impatiently against the white scales. "I need to get closer to talk to her, since you've forbidden me to mindspeak anyone," he said, glaring up at the fanged head towering above him. "I'm not giving you the Dragon's Eye until I'm absolutely satisfied she's unharmed."

Bertram hissed, but reluctantly raised his tail to allow Dai past. The firefighter's eyes stayed fixed on Virginia, without even a glance at the gold coins crunching under his boots or the fantastic hoard all around.

Perfect trust in her poured down the mate-bond as he stopped directly underneath her. "I'm here, Virginia."

Virginia met his eyes, reflecting the faith and love straight back at him, the mate-bond so incandescent she could almost see it in the air between them. "Daifydd Drake, my mate."

She took her hand out of her pocket, opening her fingers. Gold and rubies gleamed as they fell. "I give you the Dragon's Eye for your hoard."

Bertram lunged with a shriek of rage, but Dai was faster. He leapt, snatching the Dragon's Eye out of midair. Before his feet hit the ground again, they had shimmered into talons.

The red dragon spread his wings, green eyes blazing with rage and triumph. White-hot flame spilled from his jaws as he roared. *Bertram Russell, I challenge you!*

The white dragon twisted awkwardly as he aborted his charge. He eyed up the red dragon for a second, then his spines lowered submissively. *Your hoard is superior. I concede your dominance.*

I reject your submission! The red dragon lunged, claws flashing.

Bertram barely managed to twist away in time. *You—you can't do that!* He backpedalled rapidly, nearly tripping over his own tail. *I've submitted. You can't hurt me. You'd be outlawed!*

And you'd be dead. Dai's snarl made Bertram flatten to the floor in terror. *I'll kill you for touching my mate!*

"Dai, wait!" Virginia called down, but the red dragon ignored her, intent on stalking Bertram. Virginia danced from foot to foot, nearly toppling off the beam. She didn't know what happened to outlawed shifters, but she was betting it wasn't good. "No, he's not worth it!"

The white dragon made a break for the door, but the red shot a blast of fire that forced him away from it again. Bertram shrieked in pain as Dai's teeth closed with a sickening *crunch* on his throat. The white dragon writhed, futilely trying to claw at Dai, but the larger dragon pinned him down. Virginia could see the thick muscles of Dai's jaws strain, striving to choke the life out of Bertram.

If Dai killed him...Virginia took a deep breath, closing her eyes. Concentrating on the mate-bond, she threw her heart and soul into reaching her mate.

CHAPTER 16

DAI! STOP!

Dai jerked as Virginia's voice echoed in his mind. Her mental shout broke his dragon's bloodlust, leaving room for human reason to take over. He could feel Bertram's jugular pulsing under his teeth. It would be so easy to bite down...but then he'd be declared rogue. His own fire team would have to hunt him down.

A moment of revenge is not worth a lifetime with our mate, he told his inner dragon. The dragon's rage boiled in his blood...and then slowly, grudgingly, began to subside.

Dai opened his jaws, allowing Bertram to squirm free. He stared disdainfully down at the cowering white dragon for a moment, then turned his back. Stretching upward, he held out one forefoot to Virginia, claws open.

She stepped into his grasp without hesitation, and Dai carefully lowered her to the ground. She let out a relieved sigh as her bare feet touched the piled gold of Bertram's hoard. She swayed, and Dai quickly shifted, supporting her.

"Are you all right?" he asked.

Virginia leaned her head against his arm. "Never better." She reached up to his face, tracing the bruises and cuts Hugh hadn't had time to heal. "You?"

"I'm fine." He kissed her fingertips, overcome with relief. "Virginia. My mate."

Belatedly, he realized he still clutched the Dragon's Eye, now that he'd shifted back to human. He chuckled as he pocketed it, freeing his hands to embrace her tightly. "My clever, clever mate. Figuring out how to break Bertram's dominance over me."

"I wasn't sure it would work," Virginia said, slightly muffled against his chest. "But I thought, if the Dragon's Eye is *that* valuable..." She trailed off, and Dai felt her shoulders move in a small sigh, a twinge of regret passing down the mate-bond. Before he could ask her why, she pulled back a little, looking at Bertram. "What about *him?*"

The white dragon glared balefully at them both. Dai sent a wordless command to Bertram, exerting his dominance in order to force the other shifter to revert to human form.

Bertram struggled to sit upright, blood staining the front of his suit. "You won't get away with this." His voice was hoarse but outraged. Already his shoulders were settling into their usual arrogant lines. He pointed an accusing finger at Dai. "You attacked me after I submitted. I'll see you dragged before the Parliament and outlawed." His trembling finger jabbed at Virginia. "And as for *you—*"

Exactly what Bertram planned to do to Virginia, they never found out. A fiery, winged shape soared through the open doors, so incandescently bright that Dai instinctively squeezed his eyes tight shut. When he opened them again, Commander Ash stood in front of Bertram, hands clasped behind his back.

"Bertram Russell?" the Commander asked, perfectly composed.

Bertram stared at him. "Who the bloody hell are you?"

"Fire Commander Ash, of the East Sussex Fire and Rescue Service." Wisps of smoke rose around Ash's feet. Behind him, the wooden floorboards were scorched black in the outline of feathered wings. "I am the phoenix eternal, and you are in my jurisdiction."

"I don't have to answer to some jumped-up bird shifter," Bertram spat. "I am a dragon, of the line of kings! You have no authority over me."

"By birth, by blood, and by order of the Parliament of Shifters, I do. All wildfires are mine, and those who light them. You have committed arson and assault by flame, and so put yourself into my power." Holding Bertram's eyes, Ash crouched so that their faces were level. "As you have sought to burn others, so shall you yourself burn."

Bertram seemed hypnotized, frozen in place. His expression still betrayed his utter incomprehension, but his breathing sped up with primal, instinctive fear. "You—you can't burn me. I'm a dragon. I'm fireproof."

"I am the phoenix. There is nothing I cannot burn." Very gently, Ash placed one fingertip on the exact center of Bertram's forehead. "From the ashes, you will rise anew."

White light flared. Dai pressed Virginia against his chest, turning to shield her from the wash of intense heat.

"What was *that?*" Virginia exclaimed, as the blaze faded. She looked at Bertram, who was now slumped vacant-eyed and slack-jawed, but otherwise unharmed. She turned to Ash. "What did you do to him?"

The Commander rose, his expression as impassive as ever as he gazed down at Bertram. "I burned away his dragon."

CHAPTER 17

"*W*hat's going to happen to him?" Virginia said, watching the uniformed paramedics escort Bertram to the ambulance.

The former dragon shifter stumbled docilely between the muscular assistants. His face was still as blank and wondering as a newborn baby's.

"They'll look after him at the psych ward. It'll take him a while to adjust to the loss of his dragon." Dai wrapped an arm round her shoulders, holding her close. "I've seen this before. He'll be all right in the end. Just...very different."

Virginia shivered, huddling up against Dai's side. She was glad Commander Ash was fully occupied talking to the other emergency service workers that he'd summoned. She was grateful to him, of course...but right now, she'd rather be grateful from a distance. There was something deeply unnerving about a creature who could so fundamentally change people against their will.

"Is it over now?" she said hopefully. "Can we go home?"

Dai tilted his head, presumably communicating telepathically with his commander. Across the courtyard, Ash never glanced round from his conversation, but after a second Dai nodded.

"He says we should slip away now." With a touch on her elbow, Dai guided her away. "The Commander will handle the police and Bertram's relatives. It's best if we stay out of the way."

"No kidding." Virginia realized that they were headed further into the field. "Uh, Dai, the road is back that way."

He flashed her a wry grin. "I don't usually go places by road. And I noticed that there's a lovely park behind your house. Perfect for landing." He hesitated, expression turning somber. "Unless you'd rather I called a taxi. I'd understand if you've had enough of dragons for one night. Or lifetime."

Virginia laced her fingers through his. "There's one dragon I can never get enough of." She squeezed his hand, then released him, stepping back. "And I want to look at you properly, now that I'm not in terror for both of our lives. Go on."

Dai's outline rippled. Light distorted strangely around him—and then the red dragon stood in his place, posed like some heraldic beast. All the breath sighed out of Virginia's lungs. She cast a glance over her shoulder, but the police and paramedics were still going unconcernedly about their business, completely unaware of the wonder behind them.

Flashing lights from the emergency vehicles washed over Dai's scaled hide, striking gleaming red highlights from his jewel-like scales. The dragon's horned head curved downward, luminous green-gold eyes tracking her anxiously as she circled him. Virginia tentatively ran her hand across the vast shoulder, feeling the furnace-like heat emanating through the plated armor. The dragon rumbled, leaning into her palm a little. With a rustle, he spread his wings, one foreleg bending to offer her a way up to his back.

Feeling as though she'd stepped into a fairytale, Virginia climbed up. She fit herself between the crimson spines that ran down his spine, straddling the base of his neck. She felt Dai's enormous muscles shift and bunch under her thighs. Then, with a mighty leap, they were airborne.

It was nothing like her abduction by Bertram—Dai bore her up smoothly, with utmost care. His steady wingbeats rocked her as gently as if she was floating on the surface of the ocean. Virginia leaned into the motion, exhilarated by the wind rushing past and the sight of the ground falling away beneath them. She whooped, and Dai roared, echoing her delight.

All too soon, they reached the city. The lights of Brighton spread out like a shining constellation underneath them. Virginia braced herself against the spines before and behind her as Dai spiraled downward. Despite his bulk, he landed so lightly she didn't even realize he'd touched the ground until his wings folded closed. She slid off his back, wind-swept and laughing, stepping back to let him return to human form.

"Oh, that was wonderful!" She couldn't stop grinning like a loon as they walked the short distance from the park to her apartment. "Can we really do that whenever we like?"

"You'll never have to take a train again," Dai promised, his eyes gleaming with satisfaction at her reaction. "I'm afraid you're still stuck with planes for trans-Atlantic flights though." He hesitated on her doorstep. "Ah. You know, with Bertram gone, you don't need me by your side constantly anymore. If you'd prefer some privacy, I could go to—"

Virginia stretched on her toes to kiss him, cutting him off mid-sentence. "Rose was right," she said when she'd finished. She took his hand. "You really *do* overthink things."

He smiled ruefully as she led him to the bedroom. "I did make rather a hash of this, didn't I?" He caught her in his arms, tucking the top of her head under his chin. "My beautiful, brave mate. I'm sorry I didn't tell you everything straightaway."

"I didn't exactly make it easy for you." Virginia leaned against him. Even in human form, he retained that draconic heat. She snuggled closer to his chest, enjoying his more-than-human warmth against her wind-chilled skin. "I'm sorry too."

Dai was silent a moment. She had a sense of him diffidently questing at the edges of her mind, trying to untangle her mood.

"You're still sad about something," he said at last.

"No, not sad." Virginia sighed, still pressed against him. "Just a little regretful. I would have liked to examine the Dragon's Eye."

Though she couldn't see his face, she felt his puzzlement down the mate-bond. "Why can't you?"

"I'll appreciate it if you'll let me look at it, of course. But it won't be the same as being able to study it properly." She sighed again. "And it would have made a *spectacular* centerpiece to a museum exhibit."

Unexpectedly, Dai laughed under his breath. "Oh." His long, strong fingers circled her wrist, turning her hand over. "Virginia," he said, taking the Dragon's Eye out of his pocket. Without the slightest hint of hesitation or doubt, he placed the priceless artifact in her palm. "You didn't think I meant to *keep* it, did you?"

"B-But—" Virginia stammered. She stared down at the ruby-studded gold, then up into his warm, dancing green eyes. "I gave it to you, freely. It's part of your hoard. I thought dragons never gave away anything from their hoards."

"We don't." He tilted her chin up, bending his face down to hers. "But we do trade. So you'll have to give me something of equal value."

He kissed her, long and deep and slow. Virginia melted against his strong body, sweet fire singing through her veins. She could sense answering heat rising in Dai, their mutual desire echoing and ampli-fying along the mate-bond into an inferno of passion. That fire swept away all thought, all time, everything in the world except the two of them. She floated in a perfect, endless moment, aware of nothing except the blissful sensation of his mouth on hers.

Dai drew back fractionally. "There," he said, his lips brushing hers. He cupped her face in his palms, his thumb reverently stroking across her cheek. "That seems like a fair trade to me."

"Oh, no." Virginia pushed at his chest, guiding him down to sit on the bed. She stood in front of him, between his sprawled legs, and held up the Dragon's Eye so that the massive cabochon ruby caught the light. The hidden six-pointed star in its heart flared.

"I wouldn't want the other dragons to think I cheated you." She shook her head solemnly. "This is worth much more than just one kiss."

Dai's green eyes gleamed wickedly as he allowed her to push him back onto his elbows. His feet were still on the floor, his long, muscled body stretched across the bed. "Is it worth two kisses, then?"

"I'll show you what it's worth." Virginia let her robe slip off her shoulders. She still wore nothing but panties and one of his dress shirts underneath.

He watched hungrily as she slowly undid each button until the shirt hung open. She shrugged it off, and was rewarded by Dai's long sigh. His need pulled at her down the mate-bond as she slowly slid her panties down. She could feel how badly he wanted to touch her, to worship her.

Wait, she told him silently.

After all her recent fear and helplessness, she wanted to reclaim power in at least one small area of her life. From the gentle glow of acceptance and love that washed over her, she knew that Dai had sensed her need to take control, and understood it. He settled back onto his elbows obediently, though his eyes tracked her every movement with intense desire.

Virginia straddled him, feeling the thick swell of his erection even through his jeans. His hips jerked involuntarily, the friction sending delicious waves of pleasure through her.

"Wait," she said again, out loud this time. She brushed his lips with her fingertips, forestalling his protest. "It's my turn to adorn you."

"Yes," Dai said hoarsely. His eyes had gone to thin rims of gold around the wide, dark pupils. His strong hands clenched in the bedcover. "Oh, *yes.*"

Raising herself up a little on her knees, she freed the hem of his t-shirt. His abs bunched in hard ridges as he leaned forward to let her pull it over his head. Pushing him down flat again, she sat back on her heels, for a moment just admiring the gorgeous lines of his body.

Mine, she thought wonderingly, and didn't even realize she'd sent the thought to him until she felt the wave of wholehearted assent coming back down the mate-bond. He was hers; all of him, always, hers and hers alone.

Very carefully, Virginia placed the Dragon's Eye in the center of

Dai's chest, right over his heart. The gold and gems sparkled at his sharp intake of breath. The star at the center of the largest ruby danced with his heartbeat.

"Daifydd Drake, I adorn you." She tapped the artifact with one finger, shooting him a mischievous smile. "Now *stay* adorned. If you can."

Virginia bent to kiss the hollow of his throat. Her breasts brushed deliciously against the hard planes of his chest as she traced the line of his collarbone with her tongue. She ached to feel him inside her, but forced herself to stay slow and unhurried, relishing the way his breathing quickened as she worked her way down to his tight nipple.

He groaned as she grazed his nipple with her teeth, every muscle tightening. "Virginia—!"

"Careful," Virginia murmured against his tanned skin. She tapped the Dragon's Eye with one finger. "Don't let it slip."

He subsided again, though she could feel what exquisite torment it was to him to have to hold still. To have such a powerful man willingly placing himself entirely at her command was as exhilarating as flying on dragonback. Her own heartbeat sped, matching his as she worked her way yet lower, licking along his hard abs.

"Virginia," Dai gasped as she unbuttoned his jeans. His head was raised, watching her over the gold glittering between them. Awe and agony mingled in his face. He lifted his hips a little to allow her to work his jeans down. "Oh God. Virginia."

His hands fisted as she ran her tongue along the enticing grooves leading from hipbone to the base of his rigid cock. "Please. I can't take much more of this."

In response, Virginia opened her mouth and enveloped the straining head of his cock. He threw his head back with a cry, the cords of his neck standing out. Virginia swirled her tongue around him, savoring his helpless moans as she explored every inch of his thick cock. She relished filling her mouth with him, in a tantalizing preview of being filled by that rock-hard shaft. Even taking in as much as she could, he was so long she still had room to wrap her fist around the base, working him with her hand as well as her mouth.

She could feel the way she was driving him to the very edge. His intense pleasure washed over her down the mate-bond, every stroke of her tongue or hand on him echoed in her own body.

She knew the point when he could take no more, because his urgency was her own. She reared up, straddling him again. His hands coming up to intertwine with hers, his strong arms bracing her as she finally, finally slid down onto his cock.

She was so ready that the first exquisite thrust tipped her over the edge. Waves of pleasure washed over her. She rode him in a strong, swift rhythm, his hips urging her on. They mounted to higher and higher peaks of ecstasy like a dragon spiraling up into the sky, and when Dai finally arched up underneath her, calling out her name as she gasped his, it was as if they flew together into the very heart of the sun.

Sweat-drenched and satisfied in every fiber of her being, Virginia collapsed down onto Dai's broad chest. For a long, luxurious moment, she just lay there as their heartbeats slowed in unison. Then she fidgeted. The Dragon's Eye was digging into her breast. She fished it out from between their bodies.

"Well," she said ruefully, placing the artifact onto the bed beside them. "My old archaeology professor would *really* not have approved of that."

Dai's laughter rumbled deep in his chest. "I did, though." His fingers traced wondering, tender paths down her bare back. "Even my dragon thinks we got the better deal in that trade."

Virginia propped herself up on her elbows, gazing down at him. "Oh, no, no. The Dragon's Eye is worth *much* more than that." She tried to school her face into a serious expression, but one corner of her mouth tugged up despite her best efforts. "That was just the first installment of my payment plan."

"Oh?" Dai smiled up at her. His love for her was a radiant beacon in her mind. "And exactly how long does this payment plan last?"

"Well, it *is* a priceless artifact." Virginia leaned down to claim his mouth again. "How about forever?"

A NOTE FROM ZOE CHANT

Thank you for buying my book! I hope you enjoyed it. Please consider leaving a review on Amazon - I love hearing what my readers think.

The next book in the series is **Firefighter Pegasus**, which is available on Amazon now. Keep reading for a special preview...

The cover of *Firefighter Pegasus* was designed by Augusta Scarlett.

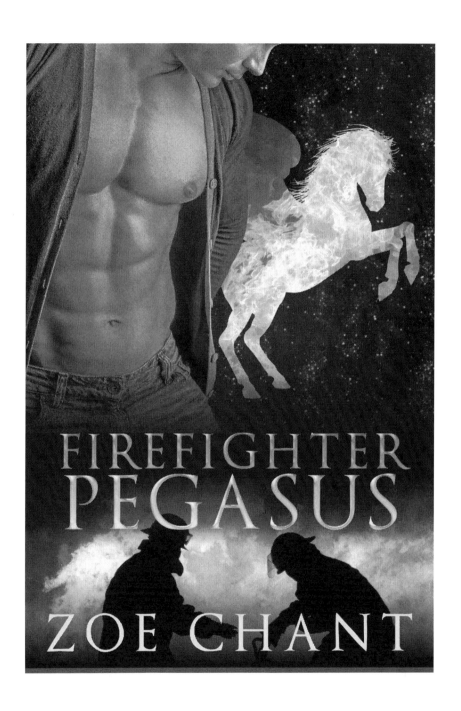

FIREFIGHTER
PEGASUS

ZOE CHANT

SPECIAL PREVIEW: FIREFIGHTER PEGASUS

Connie West was an excellent navigator. She could find her way through a fog bank at thirty thousand feet with nothing more than an altimeter and a compass. She could plot a course across three states with just a paper map, and beat pilots flying planes with the latest GPS computers. She could navigate back to an unfamiliar landing field at night with nothing more than her own two eyes.

And she could also, unfortunately, always find her way to the roughest, dirtiest gambling den in any city in the world. She'd had a lot of practice at *that* one.

She'd never been to the English seaside city of Brighton before, but it only took her an hour of searching its narrow back streets before she found the sort of bar she was looking for. She knew she'd come to the right place by the way the room fell absolutely silent the moment she opened the door.

The only patrons in the place were a small group of hard-eyed men, their glasses frozen halfway to their mouths. Connie flinched as their suspicious stares assessed every inch of her ample body.

As one, the bar patrons seemed to silently conclude that a lone, plump, nervous-looking young woman in khakis and a flight jacket was unlikely to be an undercover cop. The low buzz of muttered conversations resumed as the men turned back to their drinks and cards.

Breathing a sigh of relief, Connie edged her way to the bar. "Excuse me? Sir?"

"Well, you certainly aren't from around here." The shaven-headed bartender didn't look up from the shot glasses he was cleaning, if that was the right word for what he was doing with his gray, greasy dish-cloth. "I think you've taken a wrong turn, Yankee girl."

"I'm looking for someone." Connie showed him the well-worn photo she always carried with her. "Very tall, very loud, very Irish?"

The bartender's eyes flicked from the photo to her face momentarily. "No idea."

Connie fumbled through the unfamiliar bills in her wallet, pulling out a twenty. "You sure about that?"

The bartender gave her a long, thoughtful look. Connie put the twenty down on the bar, keeping her finger on it.

With a shrug, the bartender jerked his head in the direction of a door at the back of the bar. "You could try in there. Though if I were you, I'd go straight back home instead."

Connie sighed. "Boy, do I wish I could."

Leaving the money on the bar, she headed for indicated door. It opened into a narrow, dirty stairway that sloped steeply down into darkness. As Connie gingerly descended, a familiar Irish voice floated up the stairs.

"—the most beautiful plane you'll ever have the pleasure of laying eyes on, my hand to God. If you won't take my word for it then you can all come and see her in action at the race next week. In fact, would any of you fine gentlemen care for a little side bet...?"

"Not again," Connie groaned. She hastened down the last few steps so fast she ran straight into the door at the bottom.

"What was that?" said a man sharply.

The door opened, and an enormous hand grabbed Connie's shoulder. She stumbled as she was yanked forward into a small, smoky room.

A small group of men were seated around a green-topped table, cards and cigarettes in their hands. They started at Connie's intrusion, their cards reflexively jerking closer to their chests.

All except one man. *He* greeted her arrival with a dazzling smile—and not the slightest hint of repentance.

"Darlin'!" Connie's dad exclaimed with evident delight.

The huge man holding Connie's shoulder brandished her in her father's general direction. "This yours, West?"

"You'll not be speaking of my daughter like that, thank you," her dad said indignantly. "Or else I'll be having to ask you to step outside."

Connie twisted her shoulder free from the giant. "Dad, you *promised!*"

"Ah, now, don't be like that." Connie's dad flung his arms wide, regardless of the other men's scowls. "It's just a friendly little game."

Connie looked at the not inconsiderable pile of money already stacked in the center of the table. Even with her unfamiliarity with British currency, she could recognize they were mostly high-value bills. "A friendly game? Dad, you know we can't afford this right now!"

One of the other men at the table folded his cards, casting a level look over them at Connie's dad. "Is that so?"

"I said I'd be good for it, and I will be." Her dad gestured extravagantly at her. "With my lovely daughter copiloting my plane with me, we're a dead cert for winning the air race next week. The prize money is as good as in my pocket."

"It is *not*," hissed Connie. She cast a weak, apologetic smile around at the seated men. "We really have to go now. Sorry for any misunderstanding."

"But I'm winning!" her dad protested as she tried to tug him to his feet.

"Yeah, you can't go yet, West," said a man whose skinny, supple fingers seemed oddly out of proportion with the rest of his hands. Connie mentally nicknamed him Longfingers. "Have to give us a chance to win back our money."

"That's only fair," said another man.

A general rumble of agreement ran around the table. There was an ominous undertone to the sound that made Connie think of a pack of wolves, growling low in their throats as they closed in on their prey.

No matter how infuriatingly impulsive Connie's dad was, at least he wasn't stupid. "Ah, well," he said, starting to gather bills toward him. "Better call it a night. Sorry, lads."

Longfingers caught his sleeve. "No. You said you'd play, so you play to the end."

Connie's hand closed on the pepper spray she always carried in her pocket. It wouldn't be the first time she'd had to use it to buy them a quick escape.

Connie's dad flashed his trademark disarming, charming smile as he brushed off the man's clinging fingers. "I wish I could, my friend, but I daren't cross my daughter here. No man can change her course when she's got the bit between her teeth. Women, eh?"

Out of the corner of her eye, she noticed the giant man cast a swift, questioning glance at Longfingers. The smaller man jerked his chin in an almost imperceptible nod.

"He's been cheating," the giant announced. "I saw him. He's got cards up his sleeve."

"Now, no one likes a poor loser—" Connie's dad started.

A large man to his right grabbed his wrist, twisting it viciously. Connie's dad's protests fell on deaf ears as the thug ripped back his jacket sleeve.

A card fluttered out, landing softly on the tabletop. The black ace stared up like an accusing eye.

Connie's dad's mouth hung open for a moment. "I honestly don't know how that got there," he said weakly.

"Cheat!" roared the thug.

"*Dad!*" yelled Connie.

"Run, Connie!" Her dad ducked the first punch, toppling off his chair. "*Run!*"

The table overturned as men shot to their feet, shouting and pushing. Cards flurried into the air. Her dad disappeared into the middle of a mob of angry muscle.

Connie took aim and maced the nearest man. He screeched, dropping his cigarette to claw at his eyes. But that still left five, and her action hadn't gone unnoticed.

"Don't get in the way," growled the giant. "Ain't none of your business."

Connie tried to get him with her pepper spray, but he was too fast for her. The giant shoved her aside, kicking her feet out from under her with a casual movement. Leaving her sprawled on the ground, he waded into the fight.

Pushing herself up to her hands and knees, Connie saw her dad for moment between the angry, shoving bodies. Most of the men were just taking outraged, imprecise swings at him, but not the giant. *He moved with complete control, cutting through the crowd like a shark through water.*

Connie's blood ran cold. In a flash, she knew her dad had been set up. And she had a bone-deep certainty that he was in terrible danger.

She desperately cast around for some way to distract the mob. Her eye fell on her dropped pepper spray... and the still-lit cigarette beside it.

I can't believe I'm doing this, but...

Connie grabbed the cigarette and a handful of fallen bills. She'd never wondered how well money would burn, but the answer turned out to be 'surprisingly fast.' Connie yelped, involuntarily dropping the bills as flames licked at her fingers. They landed in a puddle of spilled alcohol and cards.

The result was considerably more impressive than she'd intended.

"Fire," Connie yelled, as loud as she could. *"Fire!"*

"What?"

"Where?"

"Hey, there *is* a fire!"

Longfingers glanced back over his shoulder. His face froze as he noticed the flames. Even though the fire wasn't *that* big yet, he suddenly looked utterly terrified.

"Oh no," he moaned. "Hammer!"

"What?" The giant's head appeared above the crowd. His expression changed to horror too as he saw the fire. "Oh, *shit.*"

The other men had lost interest in Connie's dad by now, more concerned with rescuing their money before it was caught by the rapidly-spreading flames. The giant hesitated, one meaty hand still wrapped around her dad's throat. "What about—?"

"We'll finish the job outside!" Longfingers was already bolting for the door. "Come on, we gotta get out of here! Before *they* come!"

"No!" Connie threw herself in their path. She grabbed for her dad's dangling legs, trying to wrestle his limp body away from the giant. "*No!*"

"Out of the way, girl," the giant snarled.

Connie didn't even see his fist coming. The last thing she heard as darkness closed over her was the fire's greedy, triumphant roar.

Chase Tiernach barreled gleefully at sixty miles per hour the wrong way down a twenty mph street. He lived for this—the thrill of speed, the urgency of the mission, the horrified looks on other drivers' faces as they found themselves unexpectedly confronted by a wall of bright red steel hurtling toward them.

His inner pegasus shared his elation. Driving wasn't as good as flying, but it still made his stallion prance and snort with fierce joy. Like all pegasi, his stallion was intensely competitive. There was nothing that gave it as much satisfaction as matching speed and strength against a rival, and *winning.*

To Chase's delight, an oncoming Lexus convertible tried to play chicken with twenty tons of oncoming truck. Whooping, Chase slammed the accelerator to the floor. The truck roared like an animal. Chase laughed out loud as the sports car was forced to veer off the street, ruining its shiny chrome hubcaps.

"Bastard!" the Lexus driver yelled.

Chase gave him a cheery wave out the side window as he hurtled past. "Just doing my job!"

"Alpha unit checking in," Commander Ash said calmly into the radio. The Fire Commander balanced easily in the passenger seat, barely swaying despite the fire truck's wild, bouncing motion. "Any update on the situation?"

"Observers say there's a lot of smoke," Griff's voice crackled out of the speaker. Concern thickened the dispatcher's Scottish accent. "The buildings around are close-packed, and not in good repair. High danger of the fire spreading."

"Alpha unit ETA three minutes," Ash said. "Currently proceeding east down Montgomery Street."

"Correction!" Chase spun the wheel. "Currently proceeding north up Stewart Street!"

"Please note correction," Commander Ash said into the radio. He gave Chase a level look. "Chase, *why* are we proceeding north up Stewart Street?"

"I can get us there in a minute this way," Chase yelled over the sing-song wail of the fire truck's siren. "Trust me!"

"Just when I thought I couldn't get any more nervous," muttered Hugh. The paramedic was strapped in behind Ash, and had a death-grip on his safety restraints. "Chase, are you *sure* you can get to Green Street this way?"

"Positive." Chase threaded the fire truck neatly through a slalom course of parked cars. "Up here, then nip down that little alley, and we'll pop out in just the right place."

"What little alley?" Hugh's face went nearly as white as his hair. "Chase, that's a pedestrian cut-through!"

"It's fine. There's no one in it." Chase knew that for a fact—his pegasus gave him an innate sense of where people were. It was what let him drive so fast in perfect confidence.

Ash eyed the rapidly approaching alleyway. His eyebrows drew together slightly, just the tiniest crack in his otherwise unflappable expression. "We will not fit."

"Yes we will!" Chase gunned the accelerator.

There was a horrible crunching sound.

"Mostly!" Chase added.

"Alpha Team proceeding east down Green Street," Commander Ash said into the radio. "Without side mirrors."

"May I ask if we are there yet?" John Doe said plaintively from his seat next to Hugh.

In the rear-view mirror, Chase could see that John had his eyes tightly closed. He was faintly green, which was not a good combination with his long, indigo hair.

Chase stomped on the brake, spinning the steering wheel at the same time. The fire truck lurched on two wheels, sliding sideways round the corner as it decelerated. The smell of burning rubber from the truck's tires mixed with the thicker tang of smoke.

"And here we are," Chase announced brightly.

Ash had the side door open even before the truck had fully come to a halt. He jumped down with a smooth, practiced leap. The rest of the fire team disembarked more slowly as Ash's intense, dark eyes swept the scene.

To Chase, it all just looked a mess. Thick black smoke was billowing out of the door of a shabby bar, while a small crowd milled uncertainly on the opposite side of the road. From the clouded windows, it looked like the entire building was filled with smoke. A man was collapsed on the sidewalk out front, but no one seemed to want to go to his aid.

Chase couldn't even begin to guess where the fire had started, or the best way to go about putting it out. His talents were suited to making instinctive, split-second decisions when driving, not to this sort of tactical stuff.

Fortunately, that wasn't his job.

Commander Ash gave the building the barest glance before turning back to his fire team. "Basement. There must have been a great deal of paper debris."

That was the advantage of being led by the Phoenix. He always knew *exactly* where the fire was.

"I am keeping the fire from spreading further, but we must work quickly," Ash continued. He had the slightly abstracted look that meant he was focusing on using his special talent to control the flames. "Hugh, attend to the casualties. Chase, is there anyone in the building?"

Chase concentrated. His stallion raised its head, sniffing the wind. Its ears pricked up sharply. There *was* a scent under the smoke. Something compelling, and familiar…

Chase shivered, suddenly feeling oddly on edge. "Yes. One person. A woman, I think."

"In which case, John and I will go in." Ash looked up at the enormous shifter. None of the fire team were small men, but John still loomed over them all. "We will need respiratory gear."

John nodded, heading back to the truck to unpack the breathing masks. Normally, they didn't need such equipment—Dai, their fire dragon shifter and the last member of the team, would have just strolled straight into the smoke without any protective gear at all. But he was off duty today, and miles away in London with his mate. The fire team would have to carry out the rescue the old-fashioned way… and just hope that they could reach the trapped woman in time.

Chase stared into the swirling smoke darkening the windows of the bar.

Why do I really, really wish that Dai was here right now?

"Chase. *Chase.*" He started, Commander Ash's voice finally getting through to him. "I said, get the hose ready."

"What? Oh." Chase shook himself, forcing himself to concentrate on the job instead of his strange, rising sense of urgency. "Right."

He tried to turn toward the truck, but his stallion reared up and *screamed* at him. His pegasus was frantic, hooves flashing and wings beating with agitation.

Run! Go! Now!

And abruptly Chase knew exactly who was trapped in the burning building.

"*Chase!*" Ash's shout followed him as he plunged into the smoke.

Immediately, Chase's eyes started to burn. He closed them, relying on his stallion to guide him as he charged blindly through the bar. He could feel the heat of the floor even through the thick soles of his boots.

Commander Ash's telepathic voice abruptly crashed into his head. *What are you DOING?*

Trust me! Chase sent back.

He couldn't spare the time to explain further. All of his concentration was focused on sound and touch, tiny cues that told him how to navigate safely through the burning building.

His lungs burned in his chest, but he didn't dare draw in a breath. He could taste how thick the smoke was, bitter and acrid on his tongue. Even a single lungful would put him helpless on the floor, coughing his guts out.

Holding his breath, he charged down a flight of stairs, leaping the ones that had already fallen in. Embers swirled around him. His uniform jacket and trousers protected him from most of them, but some still burned the bare skin of his neck and face. Chase barely felt the pain. His stallion danced in agitation, urging him on.

There. There!

Chase scooped her up, cradling her protectively against his chest. There was no time to check whether she was breathing. His own lungs were burning, every instinct in his body desperate to draw in air. White spots danced behind his closed eyes as he blindly raced back up the stairs.

His chest felt like he was being squeezed by iron bands. Chase stumbled, strength draining out of his legs as his body cried out to breathe. Only the weight in his arms kept him moving forward. His entire world narrowed to the single desperate need to get his precious burden to safety.

Just one more step. Just one more. One more—

He stumbled out into light and cool air. Chase collapsed to his knees, still cradling her tightly in his arms. Clean air had never tasted so good. For a moment, all he could do was blink his streaming eyes, and breathe.

Ash seized him under the arms. The phoenix shifter dragged both Chase and the woman he'd rescued further away from the burning building. "Hugh!" he shouted.

A second later, Chase felt Hugh's bare hand on his neck. A familiar, comforting warmth spread out from the paramedic's touch. The pain from his burns eased as Hugh's healing talent took effect.

"I'm okay," Chase said, jerking away. "Concentrate on *her*. Please, now!"

Hugh shot him a curious look, but transferred his focus to the rescued woman instead. Chase watched anxiously as the paramedic ran his bare hands over her throat and face. She was pale and motionless, limp in Chase's arms. Terror filled him, as thick and deadly as smoke in his lungs.

When she finally took a breath, all the air rushed out of him. He sagged in relief.

"That's it," he said to her, stroking her singed red hair back from her beautiful face. "There you are. There you are at last."

"Chase. Explain yourself." Chase had never heard Ash so coldly furious. A faint heat-haze shimmered in the air around his shoulders, in the shape of burning wings. "What is going on here?"

"Commander Ash, allow me to introduce Constance West." Chase never took his eyes off Connie's face. A broad grin spread across his own face as she started to stir. "That's it. You're okay, Connie. Everything's going to be okay."

Connie's eyelids fluttered open. She looked straight up at Chase. Her eyes widened with recognition.

"Oh, *no*," she croaked, and promptly fainted again.

Chase beamed up at the rest of the fire team. "She's my mate."

Get Firefighter Pegasus on Amazon now!

33471722R00079

Printed in Great Britain
by Amazon